heartland calamitous

heartland calamitous

MICHAEL CREDICO

HEARTLAND CALAMITOUS

An Autumn House Book

Typeset in Baskerville MT and Minion Pro
Cover design by Kinsley Stocum
Printed in Canada

ISBN: 978-1-938769-53-5
LCCN: 2019949354

All Autumn House books are printed on acid-free paper and meet the international standards of permanent books intended for purchase by libraries.

Autumn House Press receives state arts funding support through a grant from the Pennsylvania Council on the Arts, a state agency funded by the Commonwealth of Pennsylvania, and the National Endowment for the Arts, a federal agency.

www.autumnhouse.org

for Mom, Dad, and Julie

Contents

heartland calamitous

Western

No good Western begins with Indiana. Never mind how American it is: me, the Eldorado, and me having stolen the Eldorado from a One Stop in Fort Wayne.

I am trying to escape the heartland.

I want to be the type of man who would shoot another man for his wants. But I could never shoot another man. It's why I waited for an empty vehicle left running. Why it was done under the cover of dark.

We are on the road inside America when we hit a buck head-on in Cairo, Illinois. I'm beside its carcass, unable to leave it, though I'm on the lam. I mistake a Bronco for a police interceptor. The man in the Bronco offers me a knife. He says I have earned the buck's head. I saw through the bone with my eyes shut.

Where do you go from here if this is as far as you can get?

The man in the Bronco says, "Is it just you?"

No, there is a baby too. It is pressed against the cracked windshield of the Eldorado. I didn't check on it after the collision. I went to the buck and waited.

I should have run.

I thought about running when I first discovered the baby in the backseat while searching for things I could sell for gas. This was before Cairo, before Illinois. I told the baby, "Coochie coo." I sold a stag's skull for half a tank. I started the car.

I said, "Your pa must be some pa."

"My father was a drover," the baby said.

I admitted I didn't know where we were going, but we sure were.

The baby said, "Going is all we're after anyhow."

The baby isn't moving. It's gone. Still, the man in the Bronco is trying to resuscitate it.

We're all trying to figure out what's alive, what's not, and ourselves, I think.

The man in the Bronco weeps, the baby hanging from his fist like a kill.

I'm under the confluence of the rivers. I'm in the backseat of the Eldorado. The man in the Bronco is wearing expensive cowboy boots, looking at me like he needs a revelation.

I say, "What's the point of spurs in a landscape such as this?"

"Oh god. Is that all?"

"No. There is the road."

Sister

My sister was born a sheep. No. That's not right. My sister was born the same as me except for the thick, black wool. I never saw her skin and neither did anyone else. That's a tough way to be alive in the heartland.

Our parents spent her childhood trying to figure out why she was the way she was. Some folks insisted it was a sign god wasn't being loved outwardly enough.

I don't think our parents didn't love her. They were attentive, caring, and there. They were concerned, is all. "That girl—" they often said. I never once heard them finish that sentence.

When she turned eighteen, she moved to the city. She was working inside a burlesque club where once every month she stood on stage and sheared herself nude. It was art. I read about it in the papers. I showed our parents. They put me on the bus the next morning.

I snuck into the dressing room. I had a wooden cross in my pocket. She was in front of the mirror, blankets wrapped tight around her head and shoulders. No matter how I angled myself, I still couldn't see her skin.

I set the wooden cross on the floor. "For your neck," I said.

"I'm cold sometimes," she said.

"I'm here a little while if you want to talk."

"I go on in ten minutes."

That was it. I never saw my sister again.

The club was shuttered, then reopened as a bistro. Everything we think won't change eventually becomes a bistro. I understood. We move on. It's America. But I don't think my sister saw it like that. I think she felt there was nowhere else for her. I think she never once considered coming home.

She shot herself three times and that should be the end of this story. But I can't stop thinking about that number. I know the first bullet meant she wanted to die. I know the third is the one that killed her. But what about the bullet in the middle? What comes between wanting and receiving? What does it mean?

Killing Square

It's the manipulations that end you. I was told this by Sam Shaw after he learned he'd been promoted to the inside. We were on the outside of the outside in the designated smoking area. Sam Shaw said, "What's suffering worth?" He picked off the shards of animal blood that had frozen to his overalls.

I shook like I was caught in electric wires. The cigarette butt hissed when I let it drop into a snowdrift. I could hardly feel myself living, felt like I was alive as a series of smoke breaks.

Sam Shaw said, "Nothing's as dead-end as it seems."

"Easy for you to think," I said. "You're on the inside now."

I warmed my hands with the heat of the conveyor's gear motor, clenched and unclenched until my circulation was good enough that I could reach for my cutter and hand it off to Sam Shaw without either of us losing a precious something. Sam Shaw cut into a plastic clamshell that contained a dress shirt and tie combo. He pulled the tie too tight. I told him he couldn't breathe. He called himself a real professional. I lined up the next group of animals.

"You're not dressed for this no more," I said.

Sam Shaw looked at me and then the cutter. "Take it easy on me," he said, taking an animal by its pit, cutting it with no regard for the stainlessness of the shirt.

My discomfort was visible. I was almost thirty and gutless, sitting across from my mother in the kitchen in the home I'd grown up in. I'd just started my second decade of winters shoveling the driveway. I was tired from pulling doubles on account of Sam Shaw's promotion, chain-smoking to make up for the lack of sleep.

"I smell it all over you," my mother said.

"I'm in fine shape," I said.

"We didn't raise no smoker. No butcher either."

"It's temporary."

"Your father quit."

My father had smoked Parliaments until the second heart attack. This was last September. I'd asked him what it felt like and he gave me his lighter. I'd told him I guess I'm next. "No. It'll be me again," he said. He was right.

I assumed it was snow sliding off the roof when his body slumped onto the floor in the living room. I was outside checking when my mother started screaming. The ambulance pulled up. The medics asked whose blood was on my shirt.

"Animals," I said.

They strapped my father to the gurney.

"He's dead," my mother said.

"I am?" my father said.

"We don't think so," the medics said. "Not yet."

I sat with my mother in the waiting room in front of the LCD display that lists everyone in surgery like flights incoming, outgoing, and delayed. My mother began to list all the wrong things we'd eaten. I got up to get coffee. The coffee machine was next to the bathrooms. A man in a hospital gown asked how long I had left. "If it's life threatening," he said, "the nurses let you drink for free."

I'D BEEN at the killing square since college. My folks thought I'd graduated. I only had the debt. The killing square was the only place hiring for higher than the minimum. I'd passed a piss test, proved no aversion to blood.

The first shift after my father's third heart attack, I found my cutter in the pocket of another man's shirt. He said, "I figured since it was already bloody—"

"You the new Sam Shaw?"

"I don't know nothing about Sam Shaw. I'm Benjamin. I know your father's dead, and I'm sorry for it."

"It's not right."

"I started on the animals early."

"When did you get hired?"

"This morning." He unwrapped a new cutter for himself and stabbed an animal in its stomach. The screaming was unbearable.

"That's the wrong cut," I said, slitting the animal's throat.

"It would've bled out eventually."

"This isn't about eventually."

"I wasn't told any of that."

"What were you told?"

"I was told where to find a cutter. Figured the rest out. They ain't pets." He dragged the carcass to the dock. "How they get them so heavy?"

"Comfort," I said. The dock was full of steaming carcasses. "You did all them today?"

"Not much squirming. They always easy like that?"

"I think they already know," I said, thinking about my father, the way the surgeon cut him at the groin, stuck a balloon and stent into his heart, impressing my mother, disgusting me because they were using the same cutter I used on the animals.

"Look here," Benjamin said, throwing the next animal onto the killing square. There were marks around its throat like it'd tried to hang itself. I pulled its neck back until its skin was taut, until I could see an artery that would make this easiest.

My FATHER asked for his electric toothbrush. He was under observation in the ICU indefinitely, by doctors, by my mother. I was inside the house alone for the first time since I'd moved out. I tried out my old bed, got startled when the furnace kicked on, was reminded of what I was once able to sleep through. It was comfortable.

My father used the electric toothbrush while the nurse changed his piss bag. My mother tugged at my coat, pointed to the nurse's hand, whispered, "No ring." The nurse disposed of the piss bag. My mother whispered, "Beautiful." My father was working on his gums, smiling like an old dog hanging out a car window. My mother whispered, "Do you think she'd ever date a smoker?" I thought about how we'd never had a dog growing up, how my mother worried I'd get bit. My mother whispered, "Do you think she'd ever date a man with blood all over his clothes?"

I tried to quit.

I showed up to the killing square an hour early, my throat dry, my lungs tight, my heart palpitating. My sweating defied the dead-making cold.

"Finished," Benjamin said.

The nicotine withdrawal had me thinking I was. I looked over the pallets of steaming carcasses, too many of them dead too soon. "Must be you're killing different," I said.

"It's the way you told me."

"I've never done it that fast."

"I've stopped looking at them."

"I don't look at them."

"You look at them, all of them, in the eyes. I can't."

"I couldn't kill this much in a week."

"Could be your way's better. Could be how you got out."

I found the envelope taped to my locker, a notice of promotion and an increase in pay and benefits, literature on dress codes, a medical exam appointment card, and a voucher for the buffet up the street.

It was around this time I had started living in the old house because no one else was, my folks being hospital ridden. It could've been that I felt sorry for the house and it being newly vacant, and that I was looking for something. I looked through my old clothes for the right clothes for my new position. The only dress clothes I owned were the shirt and tie I'd worn for my high school graduation. They still fit. I checked myself in the mirror, figuring I should feel like I was setting foot onto a new stage in life. I felt no different. I went outside. I smoked. I thought about what Benjamin had said about how I looked into the eyes of the animals before cutting. I felt guilty.

The phone was ringing. I didn't bother running inside after it. My mother left a message: "If you're somewhere close, come to the hospital. If you can hear this—"

I went to the buffet instead, showed the host my voucher. He handed me a bib, offered to hold onto my shirt and tie. I got in line for the troughs. I asked the host if meat was all they served. "It's all you can eat," he said.

I sat down with my heaping plate of meat. I listened to everyone else eat, watched their faces turn redder and redder.

The manager tapped my shoulder. "You're not as happy as you should be," she said.

"It's just a lot."

"We get it from up the street."

"I work there."

"I am grateful for you," the manager said, starting to cry over my heaping plate of meat. "So, so grateful." She took a bite of meat. "I don't understand. It's the way it's supposed to be, and you're still unhappy."

"It's not you," I said. "I'd just rather take it to go, is all."

I set the leftovers on my father's bed. The meat had nearly greased through the bottom of the bag. The smell of it overpowered the 409 and Envirocide. My mother lunged for it. She seemed surprised by the weight. She needed both hands. She looked at me as if to ask, *Do we eat this?* I nodded yes. *We eat this.* She disposed of it carefully like a piss bag she didn't want to break open. "What's wrong with you?" she said.

"Is he better?"

"Why do you look so nice?"

"I got promoted."

The nurse walked in, asked if my father was dead.

"He won't eat," my mother said.

The nurse shook my father awake. "You have to eat or else you get the tube," she said.

"I smell meat," my father said.

The nurse lifted his blanket, found the grease on the sheets. She asked if he was bleeding.

I REPEATED, "I'm fine," over and over in the mirror the night before the exam. I'd lose my job if I wasn't fine, and I'd considered myself fine mostly until lately. Sam Shaw hadn't meant anything to me, but he meant something. I was thinking about how tight that tie was around his neck, the marks it'd left. I was scared of the inside, the trajectory.

I announced to the nurse, "I'm fine," plopped onto the examination bed. The doctor came in with the charts. "I think you're my father's doctor," I said.

"I'm so sorry," he said, forcing my mouth open, looking down my throat with a stethoscope. "Smoker?"

"Yes."

He tapped my knees with a reflex hammer. "You ever think of running?"

"Sometimes."

"Are you happy?"

"I got promoted."

"Otherwise?"

"I feel the way I'm supposed to feel."

"How are you supposed to feel?"

"Fine."

"Fine then."

"So I'm healthy?"

"These pills here are healthy. The difference will be sizeable. Take them."

I took them. I lost my desire to smoke. I had no desire left. I was feeling heavy.

It was my first time on the inside. I was lost. The walls were the kind of stainless steel you could see yourself in, and I hated it, being heavier. There wasn't anywhere to go. There was a telephone labelled RECEPTIONIST. I lifted the receiver. "Do you need help," the receptionist said.

"I think so," I said.

"What is the trouble?"

"I work here."

"Is here all you know? Is the trouble that you only know here?"

"I don't know here well enough. I'm lost."

"You are lost?"

"Very lost."

"It appears you are also late." The receptionist put me on hold. I was listening to what sounded like a jazz funeral inside a tin can. "Hello?" the receptionist said.

"I'm sorry," I said. "I was waiting for you."

"We have conflicting expectations, ours being that you show up on time and yours that I am here..."

The door appeared out of nowhere. The door led to my new office. I had a nameplate. It hurt seeing myself like that. The door shut when I sat at the desk, in front of the computer. On the left side of the screen in large green numbers was TIME. On the right side in bold red was WEIGHT. Beneath TIME and WEIGHT were three buttons: TARE, RECORD, and EXPORT. I watched WEIGHT increase all morning. I tried to stay busy by constantly moving and clicking the cursor. I opened a desk drawer looking for directions. An alarm went off. Shit. The door opened. A man thin as a stick entered. He said, "What did you say?"

"Shucks," I said.

I was embarrassed by the disparity in the quality of our clothing. His suit was expensive, though too big. It clung to him like laundry from a clothesline.

The alarm shut off.

"Did you tare?" the stick man said.

"I'm sorry," I said.

"Apologizing is not the thing you do. The thing you do, first thing, is tare."

So I did—tared—and the numbers sunk to zero, then climbed, steadily, higher.

"Bad start."

"I just started."

"Did your father die broke?"

"He didn't."

"I believe you can be more than what you are. Or you can die broke like your father. Many sons do. It is arrogance. What do you know about arrogance? About what you deserve?"

"I don't."

The stick man held up a Polaroid picture. "Do you know who this is?"

"Me," I said. That's who it was. Me. In my graduation clothes, shortly after graduation. I remember my folks posing me in front of the stage. I'm trying to smile. I tried to smile.

"You don't look this way anymore, do you?"

"I've gained some weight."

"Are you bloated?"

"Bloating is a symptom. Weight gain is a symptom."

"You're symptomatic, you're saying."

"I'm fine," I said to no one. The stick man had already vanished. The door was shut. The WEIGHT climbed. I was tired. I couldn't get myself up.

SAME THING in bed. I don't know what I was trying to relive, touching myself like I was a teenager. Nothing happened. My mother knocked. I saw she was holding a cleaver. I pulled the covers over me. I saw the night in the cleaver.

"I heard something," she said. "If it wasn't you, it'd be dead."

"Is Dad dead?" I said.

"He refuses to get better."

"Has he eaten?"

"You haven't been around."

"I got promoted."

"They give him the tube. He eats good with the tube. There's no way you can't swallow with the tube."

"Do you wonder what it feels like?"

"Choking?"

"Choking."

"I told him to think of us, and he choked. I told him I won't go back until he makes an effort to get better."

"I can see him tomorrow."

"There's hardly anything left of him to see."

He didn't look like my father anymore. He was less. He was staring at the television. "What are you watching?" I said.

"The war," he said.

"Which one?"

"I lost track."

We watched a child run for cover behind a wall of sandbags inside a garage in a neighborhood that could be anywhere. It was a drone strike. The child clutched his chest; it was too much for him. I'd never seen a child have a panic attack before. I'd also never seen bombs in a neighborhood that looked so close to mine. But it wasn't mine. The wars were always in a different hemisphere. I told my father that when he asked if I thought we were at war like them.

"Do you believe me?"

I didn't say that. The commercial did. It was selling the same pills I'd been prescribed.

"I do not know where your yellow bird has gone," a man said to a woman. "Do you believe me?"

"I do not believe you," the woman said to the man.

"You do not possess the internal strength to believe. These gifts are strength."

"They're pills."

"I call them gifts. The doctors call them gifts. Nine out of ten doctors, in fact."

"Where is my yellow bird?" the woman said, swallowing the pills.

And then the yellow bird was in the palm of her hand the entire time! And then she got carried off by the yellow bird, beaming.

My father said, "Horseshit."

I said, "Mom says you're not getting any better."

"They want me to die here. It smells like a latrine."

"They want to help you."

"They took my toothbrush. It wasn't an approved medical device. I may have gangrene."

"You don't have gangrene," I said. It was time for my pill. I took it.

My father winced. "I thought you got promoted."

"I thought you didn't want to die in a hospital."

"What's your mother think of them pills?"

"She won't come back until you get better."

"Your mother is a liar. I will die here because it's what everyone wants."

The nurse said it was time for the tube.

I hugged my father goodbye. He felt the lighter in my jacket. "Do you want to die in a hospital?" he said.

I didn't know. I gave him the lighter, and he held it like it was something he'd go on remembering me by. My mother in the waiting room, her face hidden behind a newspaper. I didn't say anything and neither did she until that night at home. She had been crying.

"It's just that I don't want to be doing this the rest of my life," she said.

"I know," I said. I meant that.

THERE WASN'T much to anything except sitting, clicking, and waiting. I was eating more, weighing more—I blamed the pills. I couldn't remember my last cigarette. I developed jowls, started wearing my father's clothes. I slept in a bed that was too small, my body sinking in the middle of the mattress, my ass touching the floor. All night I felt like I was falling. The dreams were bad too—again the pills.

I met a woman whose skin was roasted. She was wearing a toque. She had turkey-leg frills on her hands and feet. "Where are you going and why?" she said.

I was untying a porcelain gravy boat from a pier. "I don't know what I'm sorry for," I said. "But I am."

That was one Anna.

The other Anna was on her second helping of meat. I was trying to figure some things out. "Sam Shaw?" she said. "Was he the fat one?"

We were all fat. We made terrible, rolling grunting sounds at lunch. Our breasts shook. "I have breasts," I said. "Do you see what I mean?"

Anna blushed, looked down at her own breasts.

The stick man came by to inspect our portions of meat. Anna tried to say hello, but no one knew his real name.

"What's the difference between us and him?" I said.

"Wait," Anna said, shushing me.

The stick man smiled at us both, approved of our portions. "Anna," I said, realizing I couldn't stop eating. I was full and sick from being full.

"I got promoted," Anna whispered when the stick man was out of earshot.

"There's more?" I said.

"So much more," she said, reaching for a third helping.

I wouldn't ever see her again.

Same with my folks.

I HIT EXPORT on my computer at 253 pounds. The stick man held up that Polaroid picture again. "What is the difference between you two?" he said. "This you and that you? Are you happier?"

"Yes," I said. I was going by the label on the bottle. I was medically happier. "Are you happy?" I said.

"Does it seem like I am?" the stick man said.

"I've never seen you eat."

"Are you hungry?"

I admitted I was. All I had were the pills. I took them when the stick man vanished. My vision blurred. I'd have to walk home. I wasn't able to make it more than a block before needing to stop and rest. I was beneath the dark of the trees, the thicket that lined the road home when suddenly a bright light shined on me like death. The light was so bright I prayed I'd black out. I didn't black out.

"Hands up," I heard. I put my hands up. It was a sheriff and his spotlight. I lost my balance. The sheriff stood over me and said, "I thought you was an animal." He tried to drag me to his cruiser. I was too heavy for him. "Night like this a lot of folks are out for trouble," he said. "Are you out for trouble?"

"Home," I said, on my back, looking up through the tops of the trees that looked like teeth, like it was already too late.

"If you ain't much farther," the sheriff said. When I went to open the cruiser door, he aimed his shotgun at my gut. "Been looking for a guy your size. Got a match?"

"I don't smoke."

"Empty them pockets." All I had was the pills. "So you're one of them sad ones," the sheriff said. He took me home when I showed him my prescription. "Whatever's in your head, keep it in your head."

I SMELLED smoke.

The dinner table was set for three. I called for my folks. I found a burnt roast in the oven. The hospital was on fire. I watched it on the television—firehoses, gurneys, bodies. Some people stood around looking scared or praying while others seemed confused, maybe trying to figure out whether they were patients or survivors or something else. One guy turned to the camera and said, "A lot of us refused to believe this was it and didn't try to get out until it was too late."

I ended up passed out on the sofa until the next afternoon. I watched a ponytailed man stick electrodes on his abdominal muscles. He electrocuted himself and called it exercise. The ponytailed man pumped his fists with each new shock of electricity. "This is the second chance you've been asking for," he said, motioning for an increase in voltage.

I shut the television off. It was almost quitting time when I finally made it to work. The stick man was waiting for me inside the office. He was holding a Polaroid picture of a different man.

"This isn't like me," I said.

We started walking. I hadn't realized how far it was from the inside to the outside. I had come so far. I struggled to keep up with the stick man's wide, easy strides. I tried to be apologetic. Then I was back in the killing square. The stick man scissored off my clothes. A hand in my hair gently bent my head back. I saw the glint of the scaffold lights off the cutter and the silhouette of the man who was holding it. I wanted him to look at me.

Baby

I FIND A BABY UNDER THE SINK.

"Baby," I say. "What are you doing here?" The baby's caught in a glue trap, looking at me like I'm dangerous. "Baby," I say. "You don't understand." I explain my thing with bugs. That I need to set traps so that I know what I'm dealing with. Until the baby, I only caught centipedes and pill bugs. Until the baby, I thought everything was under control.

I rinse the glue off with warm water. I dry the baby with my T-shirt. I tell the baby I'm sorry. "This isn't what I intended," I tell the baby. "Can you believe I used to use poison?" The baby cries. I say the wrong thing too often.

I make a bed of blankets for the baby on the floor in the closet. I leave the closet door open.

Later that night, K. wakes me up. She asks me where I think she's been.

"How late is it?"

"It's early."

I roll out of bed, take her to the closet.

When she sees the baby, she leaps into my arms. "I was afraid you didn't love me anymore," she says. She holds the baby's face close to hers, tells me she was afraid it would end up with my nose.

"Now what?"

"You left it in the closet?"

"I didn't know where else."

"Did you name it?"

"I went to sleep."

"We can name him after your father. Or we can name her after your mother. Which is it?"

"I didn't check."

She sets the baby on its back. "Phillip!"

K. gives me the baby, gets the camera. We pose as a family in front of the bathroom mirror.

"I'm not ready," I say.

The baby is squirming and crying.

"You're overreacting," K. says.

I set the baby in the sink. "I can't."

"You're being selfish."

"I never asked for this."

"Calm down."

"It was a trap."

"Breathe."

"I am."

"Deeper."

I take too deep of a breath. The baby is in my chest, breathing inside my breathing.

"How could you?" K. screams. "Give him back!"

I exhale the baby into her arms. The baby coos and smiles. I can't take it. I inhale them both. One in each lung. I exhale a set of twins. I inhale again. They are kicking inside my stomach. I've become too heavy for my own body and collapse.

I am inside a hospital.

"The cut won't be as big as you think," the doctor says.

"We'll put you out," a nurse says. "It'll be like you're not even here."

"Turn out the lights. He's ready."

"Stop," I scream. "I don't want this."

"This is a matter of life. It's not up to you."

I wake up cradling an old woman in my arms.

"She's beautiful," the nurse says.

"Tighter," the old woman says. She has a smoker's voice. She smells like old, bad coffee. "I want to feel like I was worth it to you."

"I'm tired."

"We're all tired. That's life. If you weren't, you'd be dead." Suddenly, the old woman is sobbing.

"What is it?" I say.

"The days keep happening until one day they don't."

"That's enough," the nurse says, stuffing a pacifier in the old woman's mouth, setting her in a bassinette. She asks me if everything is how I thought it would be. I tell her the old woman isn't mine. "I'll call the doctor," she says, wheeling the old woman away.

The doctor asks me what is vital and what isn't. I'm not sure. The doctor reaches into his white coat and gives me a bottle of pills. "I recommend a handful," he says.

"A handful?"

"With water, if you like. Or swallow hard. Gulp. Like you've seen death."

I do.

I wake up in the arms of the old woman. She's still sobbing. "I'm here," I say. "It's okay."

"It's more than that. You just don't understand."

"What more do you want?"

"I already told you."

"I don't remember."

"You weren't listening. You never listen."

The nurse and the doctor are holding hands.

The nurse says, "Do you think one day that will be us?"

The doctor says, "Will we remember how we first envisioned it?"

"I could never forget."

"It's so beautiful, I know. But, nurse, take a picture."

Heartland Calamitous

I SOUGHT REDEMPTION THROUGH THE PURCHASE OF A HORSE. I was duped by the pinhooker. The horse was too damn tall. When I tried to lift myself onto it, I ended up hanging upside down from the saddle by the spurs of my boots. Either it was blood seeping from my nostrils or sarsaparilla. That wasn't the shame of it. It was a dry county, after all. But a paperboy appeared out of nowhere to say, "It must be you're afraid of horses."

"I'm afraid of no horse. I require a shorter one, is all."

"There's no such thing as a short horse. Just an ass in a horse's shadow."

I ought to have slugged him. But I had no fury with the paperboy. My fury was with the muchacho. I presumed the muchacho had strode in on a bronco of the highest caliber and ruggedness, and proceeded onto my wife, then away with my wife, Tallulah. I found our house burned down, hoofprints alien to the premises, and a note written prettily in Tallulah's cursive that read *give up.* It was clear by the hoofprints they were headed west, which is why I demanded the horse best equipped for the rigors of frontier vengeance.

The tub was all that was left after the arson. I hitched it to the too-tall horse. The paperboy helped me push the tub into the river in exchange for my purchasing several weeks' worth of papers. When the tub was in the river, I jumped in. I had learned this from canal folk. The too-tall horse remained on the bank, pulling me west. I didn't pay the paperboy what I had promised. I didn't feel guilty for it either. I was adrift, out of earshot of his wails and curses.

It was dark. I was scared. Sure. And maybe it was the right moment for prayer. But I don't pray. I expect. I expected that once the too-tall horse and I made it to the West the fear would dissipate, if only because of the increase in temperature. Still, my stomach churned. A bucolic sick. There were eyes all around us, blinking. The eyes looked hungry. The dark looked hungry. I was too. Do you know what I mean?

So I swallowed a fish hook, but not completely. I took hold of the line, wrapped it several times around my wrist so there was some give to it in case whoever's line it was pulled at his reel, thus ripping out my gullet. I stumbled over the side of the tub. I was on land again, looking up at the too-tall horse. We followed the line to a pier. An old-timer was asleep in a chair on the pier. The fishing pole was staked between his legs. He woke up when I reached for it. I couldn't speak. I pointed to the hook lodged in my throat. The old-timer pulled out a long list of names, began to read them one by one, told me to say so if any of the names were mine. I wasn't any of them. "Well you've got nothing to worry about then," the old-timer said. He ripped the hook out of my throat. No blood. No pain. I was fine. The old-timer said, "If your first thought's to look up to the big blue sky and say something, don't bother. It's no miracle. It's timing."

"Yessir."

The old-timer went back to sleep. I was still hungry. I took up the fishing pole, reared back to cast and hooked onto something behind me. A bucket. The old-timer's bucket. I'd sent it flying through the air and into the river. The bucket had been full of white-feathered wings. They struggled in the water. Sank. The old-timer was still asleep. I decided to leave without saying anything to him about the drowned wings. As I whispered up to the too-tall horse that it was true what they said about the frontier being different from anywhere else that a man was used to, all these fish flew out of the river. It was a hell of a thing to see winged fish looking down at you like that. You really get to feeling low and yellow-bellied.

"You kicked the bucket," the old-timer said.

"I didn't kick the bucket," I said.

The old-timer asked for my rifle. I told him I had no rifle.

Downriver a cowboy rode his slowly wading horse through the water. The old-timer turned to me and said that horse there was about to turn cripple. The horse squealed, bucked below the surface of the river. The cowboy sank along with it. The old-timer stopped me from trying to save him. "He's already drowned," the old-timer said, crossing his name off the list. He filled up his bucket with water and swigged. He offered me a swig. But I was too afraid of tasting the drowned cowboy to drink.

ANOTHER COWBOY and a woman called Clem saved my life from some Chickasaw that had lassoed me captive on account that I fit the description of a cannibal they were sore at. The chief displayed a chunk of skin and sinew and muscle that had been bitten off his arm. I agreed that it looked bad, disagreed it was I who bit into him like that. Still, the chief and the rest of the natives decided I deserved a similar cut, after which I was to be hanged.

It was then that the cowboy and Clem rode up requesting safe passage for them and theirs. They saw how sorry I looked, my hog-tied ass being poked and prodded. The chief gesticulated wildly, spoke directly into the gash in his arm as though it was another person. I was going to be made an example of. Clem whispered something to the cowboy. Then the cowboy explained to the chief that it would be unfair for one man to take another man's selfhood without certain proof of wrongdoing. "That would be un-American," the cowboy said. The Chickasaw rolled their eyes. The gash in the chief's arm spat blood into the dirt. Clem forced an apple into my mouth. She displayed the teeth marks for all to see. I simply wasn't a match. I wasn't the cannibal. The chief put the gash up to my ear and it said something I couldn't understand. I was let free.

The cowboy and Clem started me drinking. We mumbled a toast to the West. I asked where we were exactly. "Missouri," the cowboy said. In fact, I had called them both cowboys, then upon realizing one of them was a woman, I called her ma'am. She pulled her gun on me, demanded that I call her by her Christian name or she'd shoot.

"I'd be dead without you both," I said.

"How come you didn't escape on your horse?" the cowboy said. He mounted it with ease.

I told him to stop, that the too-tall horse was mine to ride only.

"Seems like she hasn't been ridden much at all," he said. "Besides, she likes it." He rode her in circles. Clem said that his riding her was a condition of my following them to Montana.

"What is in Montana?" I said.

"The rest of the West," Clem said. She lifted her pants leg to show me a two-hole scar on her upper thigh from a run-in with a prairie rattler and then showed me the belt she made from its hide.

I watched the cowboy ride the too-tall horse to where it seemed like the sky and the earth met. I felt it symbolic of all the possibilities of the West. It made my heart sick thinking of Tallulah and all her possibilities with her new beau. Clem lassoed me onto her horse, slapped me on the buttocks. We rode to an acre full of bovine, their bovine. They were drivers.

"I'm still drunk," I said.

"Are you seeing spots?" the cowboy said.

"Do you want to drive?" Clem said.

"Steer," I said.

"Yes," the steer said.

I got sick in the dirt. The steer laughed. I mentioned that I was hungry. Their eyes were big and brown and sad. Clem lifted me off the ground and back onto her horse. I held onto her by the two-hole scar. We watched as above us a winged fish slowly descended and landed on a steer. "What in tarnation?" she said. When the steer swatted at it with its tail, the winged fish took to the air again.

CLEM AND I tried to make love among the steers, with the cowboy watching from atop the too-tall horse, but I was hurting for Tallulah still. "The way steer hurt for peacefully grazing on the hearty, limitless greens of West Texas?" Clem said. "Don't you realize the sky was born from god himself for fornicating under? Don't you ever imagine your woman making love to another man? As we make love I will imagine your woman making love to the muchacho."

"You don't know either of them."

"I am imagining myself making love to the muchacho."

I pulled the blanket over my head. Clem gave me her gun. I asked what for. She got up, plumb naked, and fetched her guitar. "Here's one for the cold-blooded persistence of our pasts," she began. "It goes a little something like this:

> Where you can go farther and see less,
> Where there are more creeks and less water,
> Where there are more cows and less milk,
> Where there is more climate and less rain,
> Where there is more horizon and fewer trees,
> Than any other place in the Union
> Beautiful West Texas, what do you think?"

The steers began to stampede. Clem called out to the cowboy. We scrambled for our clothes. There was blood everywhere. I didn't know where it was coming from. I stepped on a human tooth, a human canine tooth. Clem's guitar got trampled to pieces. The cowboy limped toward us. The too-tall horse looked at me sorrowfully.

"What happened?"

"She threw me off."

"Can you feel your legs?"

"They hurt."

Clem started up again with her song, this time a cappella:

> "Plenty of grapes and nothing to drink,
> Plenty of creeks and no water on hand,

No oats for your horses but plenty of land.
Plenty of ponies, none fit to ride.
Plenty of poverty and some little pride."

My fly was down. I caught Clem looking down at my down fly. The cowboy caught me catching Clem looking down at my down fly. "What do you suppose scared the steer?" I said.

"I think it was the coyotes," the cowboy said.

"Have you ever been to West Texas?" Clem said.

"Should I have been to West Texas?" I said.

"Only thing you'll find in West Texas is that you've got to find a way to get out of West Texas."

"Someday."

"Someday."

"Someday," I said, all by my lonesome. The cowboy and Clem were gone. They had taken the too-tall horse with them.

I STUMBLED around a place quiet as a ghost town, but it wasn't. There were bodies, parts of bodies—torsos, insides, and appendages—torn up, discarded, and what have you. I tripped over somebody else's feet. The toes had been gnawed to the bone. Coyotes? I had never seen a coyote before in my life. I still had Clem's gun.

I started knocking on doors. There was an answer at the saloon. A hand reached under the door and touched my boot. "What a delicious hand I have," I heard spoken from inside the saloon. "What a healthy and hearty supply of marrow and blood. Do you like the taste of skin? Do you like cellulite? Yum!"

"Let me in," I said.

"Because you are hungry?"

"Please," I said. I grabbed the hand. It wasn't attached to anyone. I threw it away. I cried out Tallulah's name. I cursed her. I sobbed a little. That's when the saloon door opened. The bartender pulled me in. I helped him board the door back shut.

"I needed to be certain you weren't one of the hungry."

"The who?"

"The cannibals."

The old-timer was at the bar downing shots of whiskey straight from a whiskey barrel. He threw the empty shot glasses against the wall. He couldn't hold his liquor. It seeped from his body, onto the floor.

"I think it's Judgement Day," the bartender said.

"Then why are you so afraid?" the old-timer said. "It's out of your hands, isn't it? Or is that the trouble? You can't control this."

The bartender said he was feeling faint. I helped him to the backroom. There was a cot and a body. The body was missing a hand. I smelled rot. I lay the bartender on the cot. I covered the body with a sheet. It was the best that I could do.

As I watched the old-timer drink, I really started to miss the dry county. "Looks like you got the blues," he said. "Which isn't the worst thing you can have around here." He handed me a washboard. He told me to play the blues. There was another stampede outside. The sloshing of blood and the cracking of bones. Then quiet. Then chewing.

The bartender was devouring the body in the backroom. He offered me an intestine when he saw the horror on my face. I shot him point-blank. The old-timer sighed, opened his bag, which was full of winged fish. He plucked off a set of wings and stabbed them into the bartender's back. The bartender's eyes opened wide. He floated up through the ceiling. The old-timer went back to drinking. I told him I couldn't stay here like this. I had a vendetta, a reason to keep going. "No matter the predicament outside?" he said.

I took a peek. There were hundreds of them. "I'm hungry," I said.

"Dead."

"Shucks. No matter."

The old-timer wrapped a piece of cloth around the end of a broken off chair leg, soaked it in whiskey and lit it on fire. He gave it to me. And a winged fish too.

"I might die," I admitted.

"Yes. You will."

"What about you?"

"I have all the sustenance I need right here."

The old-timer boarded the saloon door shut behind me. I ran toward the dead with the torch. They quickly split apart, providing easy passage as they cowered. I caught a couple on fire by accident. I apologized. I ran until I couldn't anymore. I was in the woods. I thought I was alone. Then I saw a snake. I emptied the gun into it.

A woman began shouting, "He's dead. You killed him!" I found her holding the dead man in her arms. I asked her where I shot him. She lifted his shirt, but he wasn't shot. It wasn't my fault he was dead. I told her it looked like he was bitten into. "Don't say that," she screamed. "Stop it." She began swinging at me. I took hold of her wrists.

"We got to get out of here," I said. "Do you understand?"

She said my name; I said hers and some curses too. The dead man woke up and bit a chunk from her bosom. I struck him upside the head with the gun. His eyes fixed on me. And then her eyes fixed on me. They were looking at me with their teeth.

"I will shoot you both. Believe me when I say I will shoot you." I pulled the trigger. No bullets left. It was a real calamity. All I had left was the winged fish. I plucked off its wings. The dead man charged at me first. I stabbed the wings into him. He groaned, charged at me again. I put my hat on him, pulled it down over his eyes. The woman thought he was me and latched onto him with her teeth. The wings began to flap. They took off attached to each other. I began to think, what if I had given up like she wrote? What then? I got down on my knees and expected.

I THOUGHT I was broken down for good until I followed a set of hoofprints to that place I told you about earlier, where the sky met earth. What would you say if I said it was the Ozarks at twilight? The horse was lying next to a watering hole at the foot of a mountain. The water wasn't clear. It was reflective. I was looking at the horse through it. It wasn't the too-tall horse. It was a good horse, is all. I told it that. Good horse. I noticed it had been bitten into too. Our blood was dripping into the water. The water turned orange and then purple and then black as the night we had to survive. The Western cold set on us. I lay next to the horse for warmth. I felt its eyes on me and its breath. "Be ready," I said. "Come morning we'll be riding."

Postwar: Lake Michigan

"I SAW HIM IN OUR POOL AGAIN," K. SAYS.

"It's hot out," I say.

"It isn't his, is the thing."

I look out the window. The trees are all gone. We lost them to the zoning commission. It is just sky now. I feel aloft.

"I mean it. He was here and shouldn't have been."

"I know. But it's late."

"You don't believe me."

"I can't do anything about it."

She gives me a flashlight. "It's not really a home if anybody is welcome."

"There's no one else."

"We can't teach our kids to swim with strangers."

"I can't swim. There are no kids."

I find the body floating in the pool. I use a rake to poke at it. It floats to the middle of the pool, out of reach.

K. hugs me from behind, I feel that she's naked. "Do you believe me now?" she says.

"Get dressed," I say.

"He can't see us." She kisses the back of my neck. She tells me too late to come inside her. I come into the water.

I AM on the sidewalk smoking a cigarette when a stranger asks what I do.

"Quality assurance."

"I always wondered."

"My father told me this is where I will die. He wouldn't have it any other way."

"I never knew my father. Only time I scared a man is when I was born."

"I was born for quality assurance, I guess."

"Is it numbers?"

"And graphs."

"I'm not smart, but I have good hands."

"I thought I would be doing something else by now. Anything else."

"Is this government work?"

"We're the bombs. Yes."

"Do you know who for? I can't keep up."

"I only know the metallurgy."

"I don't read the paper as much as I used to."

"We're mostly classified, I can tell you. Anything else, I can't. Do you understand?"

"Do you understand what will happen when all the bombs are made?"

"We also build planes here," I say.

It won't ever end.

We laugh.

K. SAYS, "My sister's pregnant again." She buries her face in a pillow.

"Everyone agrees you're the good aunt."

"You missed dinner."

"I've been working overtime. Two wars right now. Officially."

"I was the only one there who wasn't a parent. The only one drinking wine too. When I spilled some on my shirt, my sister said, 'Oh, that's cute.'"

"She didn't mean anything by it."

"I made a wish tonight."

"What for?"

"I said out loud, 'I wish,' and that's it. And nothing happened."

"That's it?"

"It was 100 degrees today, and I couldn't even go swimming."

"He's too far in."

"You're not the man I married. I'm trying to figure out who you are."

"I'll move him in the morning."

"I couldn't drown in my own damn pool if I wanted to."

I AM standing at the edge of the pool. It has been a few days. I expected dissolution, but the body is only getting bigger. I have a rope. It takes me dozens of throws before I hook a limb. I put on dish gloves. I flip the body over. This isn't a drowning. There's no face. This was a bludgeoning.

WE MARRIED the summer we met. A prominent journalist had just been beheaded overseas. The wars ramped up again. A surge. I was young enough that I could still join the army. For no reason other than it was something else, I filled out the paperwork at the recruitment center. The soldier looked it over. He laughed. He unbuttoned his shirt, revealing a tattoo of a MOAB bomb across his chest. He was hairy all over except for the bomb, which had been thoroughly plucked or waxed. "You're already as important as any of us," he said, tossing my application into the trash.

A PLANE has gone missing over Lake Michigan, a model on which I had signed off. Production comes to a halt. I am home early.

K. says, "Imagine just vanishing."

"I know."

I am looking out at the body on the patio. I expected disintegration, evaporation, even. Total decomposition. A lessening. It is growing instead. The flies are building an entire civilization inside him.

"IF YOU ask me," the stranger says. "I say you killed him."

"I didn't," I say.

I THROW a tarp over the body. I try to kill the flies with bleach.

K. says, "I like it when you're home."

"I can't figure out how it happened."

"Gone is just gone sometimes. Maybe it's what he deserved."

"Do you think he tripped and hit his head?"

"What's important is it wasn't his pool to go wandering near." She is holding me again.

"Stop," I say.

"I'm pregnant," she says.

My shoes are covered in blood. "I think it's you."

"Baby," she says. She collapses. I hold her hand in the ambulance. The paramedic gives me a tissue for my shoes.

SHE IS still out after surgery. I am bedside when the doctor walks in.

"Are you the family?"

"Yes."

"What do you know about the cervix?"

"I'm not sure."

"Think of it as a way out. What happened is it was about the size of this." She makes a fist.

"The baby?"

"That's a different kind of handful."

"Cancer?"

"Granite," the doctor says, pulling a rock out of her pocket.

K. WAKES up. I put on the television. War. Wooden boxes unloaded off planes.

"I'm not afraid to bring anything into this world."

"There isn't anything being brought in."

She cries until the nurse IVs her back to sleep.

I stay up until the television is postwar. Lake Michigan. Everyone is desperate for wreckage, dressed in their wetsuits, sucking on their snorkels. It is the same question over and over: how does someone just disappear?

But what if it was an escape? A half mile of elevation, see an opening, go.

One of the would-be rescuers keeps looking at the sky. I wonder if we have the same lonely feeling, if we're thinking what the pilot thought when he set the throttle to full.

Redbird

BEGINNING THIS DAY AND TIME FORWARD, I AM NO LONGER IN LOVE WITH THE REDBIRD.

I am inside a bank. I am carrying an envelope. I am liable to do anything. I always believed that. I told the redbird, too, that with me you just never know.

The redbird left me for a man shaped like a babushka doll. How can you love a man so round, whose arms are always at his sides?

I was trying to open up to her the way she wanted me to. She said it's what's inside that's important. What's inside the inside and what's inside the inside of the inside.

I am feeling unwell.

I hold up the envelope. I shout this is a holdup.

A slouching teller offers me a stamp. I explain that this envelope is filled with anthrax.

I expect panic. They are resigned instead.

"No longer can I pretend the unsavory parts of my life may someday resemble sweetness," the slouch says. He declares himself ready for the poison. So do the others.

"I flipped my Word-A-Day desk calendar to this day and saw the word *grievous* and tried to use the word *grievous* in a sentence and realized the sentence is life."

"I have been reduced to yearning for a blanket of heavy, impenetrable sod."

"I go home and attempt not to decompress but to decompose."

"I'm unable to reminisce."

"I ache on account of it being not just I, but all of us, aching."

I am really missing the redbird. Poison isn't poison enough. It is talcum powder in this envelope. I am fraudulent. The room ingests it gleefully like a communion wine.

"Bless you," the slouch says.

"Bless you."

"Bless you."

They incorrectly feel at peace. My intention was panic inducement, suicide by cop, the redbird flipping the television on and saying to the babushka doll, "I knew."

They think they are going to die like I thought I was going to die.

I remember the redbird asking me why it was so hard for me to let people be happy. I remember her calling me a *harvester of souls*. Her insides were somewhere else.

"I would like to be happy," I say.

The slouch scoffs. "Life loses its luster with living," he says, a puff of talcum escaping his mouth.

I watch for emergency lights, for authorities with weapons brandished.

Everyone moans, affecting stomach pains and death rattles.

We have been free willed into oblivion.

I hear the redbird say, "Have you ever tried believing in something?"

"I'll believe anything," I say.

"I don't believe you."

I plug my ears.

"Listen to me," she says. "When is the last time you really held something close?"

"Yes."

"Can you hear me?"

"A long time ago."

The slouch joyously complains about how upset his entire body's become. He collapses to the floor. They collapse to the floor. Then I collapse to the floor. We stop breathing until we can't not breathe any longer.

Pines

THEY WOULDN'T ACCEPT THE EMBARRASSMENT OF LOSING THE BOY TO A BEAR, SO THEY MADE THE BEAR THEIR NEW BOY. Pa dissolved a couple of Ma's Ambien in a bucket full of tonic water. The bear lapped it up, fell asleep. Pa strapped him to the bed. Ma kissed his warm, matted face.

There were worse ways to be a happy family, the folks decided.

They named him Jeremiah, Also.

Jeremiah, Also was dreaming up a different inverted world. He was still a bear, of course, but he was gently caressing the cheek of a young girl in a flowery spring dress. He felt feral. He admitted to her it was love. She lifted her skirt, revealing a bear trap. Her teeth were beautiful; he couldn't turn away from them. He wondered if she was looking at his the same way. He became nervous, ashamed, thinking of the obscene lengths of his canines, the fist-sized gap between his canines and his molars. If the young girl moved to kiss him, then what? He was suddenly unable to open his mouth.

GRAM HAD been dying by complications from heart disease for over fifty years. In her words, she'd been alive with a death sentence most of her life, never really able to live.

The first thing she said to Jeremiah, Also was, "That nose!" Though he'd shrunk considerably from the 2,000-calorie-a-day diet the folks supplied him, his snout hadn't changed. Another thing was the redness of his flesh. His skin reacted badly to Ma's wax sessions. Pa said it was only rosacea or acne, a temporary irritation.

Jeramiah, Also was just entering high school and unsure of himself. He struggled with eye contact. He constantly, viciously bit at his claws. Once a girl called Susanna said hello to him unprompted and he felt himself pee a little. Ma called it tinkling, said it meant he was happy. Pa switched the sheets to plastic.

But Jeremiah, Also wasn't happy.

The last thing Gram said was, "I have reason to believe you don't share blood with any of us."

To the shock of most everyone at the funeral, Jeremiah, Also dragged her casket from the church to the grave himself, with only his teeth.

Susanna said to him later, "I lost my grandmother too." He waited for her to move closer. Then he quit waiting.

Pa announced the divorce the day Jeremiah, Also found the shoebox of photos of Jeremiah, Devoured. Ma snatched them from him quick, sobbed. Pa slammed the front door shut and was figured to never be heard from again.

Jeremiah, Also noticed stubble all over his chest and legs and arms. Ma could muster no energy for waxing. He was clumsy with the razor, making tiny cuts all over his body until he looked like a red-and-white polka-dotted teddy bear.

He wanted to ask Ma, "Do you love him still?" Instead he growled, "It's all my fault," and locked himself in his bedroom. He stuck his paw down his throat, forcing himself to vomit. He hoped he could return Jeremiah, Devoured, restore things the way they had been. He choked up lips, still colored with lipstick, still tasting sweet, soft. He remembered Susanna's braids, the way it felt when they untangled in his stomach.

MA WALKED in on Jeremiah, Also downing the last of the Ambien. She knocked the empty bottle from his paw, screamed, "Jeremiah," then, "I'm so tired." Her non-specificity hurt him, made him feel like an overdose was the right thing. Ma got the shakes, collapsed and crawled downstairs to the kitchen. He followed, his steps heavy as his eyelids. He tried to grab her but fell. The weight of his upper body paralyzed everything from the waist down. It felt like he was beginning to evaporate.

Ma boiled milk in an attempt to stave off the rest of withdrawal. When the milk was gone, she lay in flakes of lavender, gardenia, and jasmine. Nothing worked until Pa came back for his gin and Ma crushed him upside the head with the bottle. Pa lay unconscious next to Jeremiah, Also. Ma set herself gently over both bodies. Jeremiah, Also felt her weight. Her breathing was heavy. His got lighter.

THE CHILD wore a bearskin rug, held a plastic, pumpkin-shaped pail full of candy. "In the pines," the child whispered.

That's where Jeremiah, Also was. "What happened last night?" he asked the child.

"It's still last night," the child said. "Are you hungry?" The child unwrapped a candy bar, forced it into Jeremiah, Also's mouth.

Jeremiah, Also couldn't chew it or swallow it or speak.

"Are you cold?" the child said, removing the bearskin rug from himself and draping it over Jeremiah, Also.

The child was naked and began to shiver.
Jeremiah, Also pulled the child toward him, held him.
The pines were eternally tall and evergreen.

Heartland Aquatic

I FIGURE TWO THINGS WHEN SHE SCREAMS: either she has slipped in the shower trying to cut her toenails, striking her head against the metal spigot or she is writhing on the imitation sheep-curl bath mat, choking on her toothbrush because she has this thing about needing to brush the little bumps on the back of her tongue. Instead, K. has turned into a fish.

I try to lift her out of the tub. She slips through my fingers, is swirling in the whirlpool above the drain. I plug it. We align eyes. I tell her I am sorry for how everything has turned out. I guide her into a ziplock baggie. I carry her around the house like a carnival prize, reminding her of everything we have together. The furniture. The knickknacks. The glue traps in the corners of the rooms we set out because I wanted to be sure all this was ours and only ours, and all we ever catch is dust and hair and sometimes roly-polies that close up into little balls when they are stuck and afraid.

I am trying to keep still but I am trembling and the waters are getting rough.

I would like to explain. I could say she is visiting her folks in the country. But her folks are dead. I was at both funerals. I mean it was the same funeral. They died the same time, same place because love is eye for an eye in the heartland. She asked why there were so many windows in the funeral home. I lied and said that they were one-way windows. We could see out, but no one could see in. I stood outside to prove it to her. When she pressed against the window and waved at me, I tried to not react.

"Nothing?" she said.

"Nothing," I said.

I could say there was another man. There is always another man. Everyone would agree. "Things change, and people change," they would say, and I would say, "Yes, but I never expected it, I never saw it coming," and they would say, "It only seems that way now." Then they would ask about the boy.

The school bus is outside. I meet him at the door. When he sees the fish he asks me what we will name him.

"It's a her," I say.

"How do you know?" he says.

I put my hand over his mouth. K. and I agreed this is a conversation I can't have without her.

I pour her into a glass bowl. We sit at the kitchen table watching her swim. Circles and figure eights. I wonder if it feels like she is getting somewhere, and if she is, what does that mean for me and the boy?

"Can I feed her?"

"She isn't hungry."

"Where's Mom?"

"Go to your room."

I fall asleep thinking of us boys stuck here without her.

In the morning she is gone, belly-up inside the fishbowl. The boy is on the floor, still asleep. I try to step over him without waking him. But when I start to cry, he starts to cry.

I carry the glass bowl to the bathroom. The boy follows

and for a moment I wonder if that is the right thing. But he is hers the same as me. I ask him if he wants to say something. He waves goodbye.

I empty the bowl into the toilet. The initial splash of her body makes it seem like she is still alive. The boy grabs onto me. "It's okay," I say. "She is dead."

I am trying to not believe this, imagining her swimming up through the plumbing and into my body. "You can have whatever part of me you can fit into," I say before flushing.

She doesn't go all the way down. The toilet overflows. The bathroom fills up with water. The scales that wash off her body look like tiny blonde heads. We must look like giants to them, but we are swallowed up and carried away just the same.

This Boy Here. He Will Kill You.

I WAS ON THE EDGE OF A COASTAL BLUFF FEELING BAD FOR A BUOY. It had no purpose other than being there in case something went wrong. I was hoping something might go wrong for this pack of kids in the water yonder. Loud and rude as all get out. I wasn't being cruel. I wasn't thinking they should drown. No. They were kids, is all. But what about almost? It had almost happened to me. For three months, I had a fixed address in Muncie. I lettered back and forth with a woman in Huntington. She wrote that she had a pool, that it was a nice pool, real clean, pumps and filters and chlorine. Sometimes she would swallow the chlorine. She wrote that it was pleasant to have a clean mouth, that she desired to clean-mouth another person, that if I was serious for her, I could swallow the chlorine too and clean-mouth her while her folks were away on business in Fort Wayne.

I wasn't much for the water. My father promised that he would teach me to fish as soon as he was done soldiering for the country, but soldiering was the last thing he ever did. Same with swimming. I had dreams of my mother swimming. I was the last thing my mother ever did. Still I was a man and in Huntington there was a woman. I lettered back that I was on my way. She was in the pool when I arrived. "Do you know who I am?" I said. She shook her head yes. The water rippled. My heart rippled. She went just below the surface. I bent down to kiss her. But with water the distance isn't ever the way it looks. I bent and bent and by the time our lips met I was as good as dead. She pulled me out before I drowned. She sucked the water out of my chest. She tasted clean and then so was I.

"I don't think this is going to work out," she said.

"But I am here and I'm a man."

"You're a man and there's this taste in my mouth I can't spit out."

"I brushed my teeth."

"I can't always be there to save you," she said. "I'm sorry."

I got choked up thinking about the distance I had come to be with her. It wasn't enough. I was a man and that meant I needed to keep going, so I bowed my head, lifted my heavy heart, and continued east to god knows where.

That pack of kids came no closer to drowning than I did sleeping that evening. They were safe on the shore. I was glad for them like any decent man would be. And like any decent man would, when I saw a yappy dog fly over my head and off the cliff and into the water, I jumped in after it. I realized that the Huntington woman had been right about her not being able to save me like she said she wouldn't. I was struggling in the water with the yappy dog in my arms. The pack of kids shouted that I should swim to the buoy. I shouted back that I couldn't. I felt my lips turning blue. My eyes welled up so bad I couldn't see anymore. I focused on the yappy dog's bad breath to stay conscious. Somebody threw us a rope. I clung to it with one hand, the yappy dog with the other. We were lifted out of the water by an angry man who kept screaming, "Forget the damn dog!"

"I haven't almost died for nothing," I cried. But when I was safe on the bluff again, the angry man took the yappy dog and threw it back into the water. I tried to jump after it. The angry man caught me by the collar, slammed me down and stabbed me. I woke up smarting all over. The yappy dog's body was floating in the water like a second buoy. I was sitting on the edge of the bluff with an elderly woman. She was knitting a sweater. It was the heartland and winter was always coming. I realized I was shirtless and that I was sewn shut where the knife had gone in.

"It looks to me like you've never been to Ohio before," she said.

"No ma'am," I said.

She held out the knife. "You'll need this if you want to do Ohio right."

I held it by the blade. "I want to do Ohio right," I said.

Myself, I couldn't see much difference between Ohio and Indiana except for their lake being theirs. Chicago had its claim on Lake Michigan because they had the culture and the economy, so no Indianan would ever worry them over it. We didn't worry over anything north of Route 6. The air still smelled like calf shit and steam engines and corn. I walked along the lake for as long as my wound and hunger would allow. I collapsed in front of a tall steeple. Thank god. The clergy always ate better than they let on.

Father leered at me from the altar. "It isn't Sunday."

"I came for charity."

"Is charity what you believe in?"

"I believe in all of it."

"Are you even American?"

"I am Indianan."

"Are you an urchin?"

"I am a man."

"With money?"

"No money."

"Talent?"

"I'm not sure."

He pressed me against a concrete Jesus, patted me down, found the knife. "In whose name would you have killed me," he said. "And for what?"

"It's my own blood on that blade," I said.

He left the knife to soak in a bowl of holy water. He brought me a plate of goose liver bits and a couple bottles of sermon wine.

"I don't drink," I said.

"Me neither," he said, opening the first bottle.

The combination of goose liver, wine, and watching the votive candles made me nauseous. I lay down in a pew. "I don't think I've ever been saved," I slurred.

"That's tough," Father said, handing me the clean knife. "But this is tougher." He went over to a stained-glass angel and pointed to its nether regions. "What do you know about penetration?" he said.

"Do you mean of a man or of a woman?"

"This is a symbol. This is symbolic. I mean this symbolically." When he bellowed penetration, it echoed throughout the church. I could hardly stomach it. I held the knife up. I tried to aim higher than the nether regions so that if I made a mistake, I wouldn't kill Father. No good comes for sermon-winedrunk men who kill clergy.

I threw the knife. It stuck to where it was supposed to.

"Christchristchristchistchrist!" Father said. "Now this is worth something."

We set out the next morning to find a man who paid $200 for the skills I had demonstrated. Father said we would split the profit. He mentioned a finder's fee. "Where once you were lost you have now been found," he sang, as we walked through a dense field of corn.

Then we were in the plains. Then we were in the wilds. Father knocked on the door of a cabin that was secluded deep in the thicket. A woodsman answered. He crossed himself and Father crossed back. He gave him a bottle of sermon wine. The woodsman read aloud the year on the label and scoffed. "This boy here any better?" he said.

Father laughed. "This boy here. He will kill you."

My ears turned hot. It should have been because of the mention of *kill*. But what hurt was being called boy. "Sir," I said, politely. "I am a man. I could serve my country if I wanted to."

"Do you even know which war we're on?"

I lowered my head.

"Never mind," the woodsman said. "Show me your knife."

"First, the money," Father said.

"There's money and another thing. I'll meet you out back."

We were in a clearing behind the cabin. Father leaned against a pile of logs and swigged from the bottle of wine. I sat in the grass, waiting for the woodsman to reappear. When he did, he was nude. But not regularly nude. He was covered in hair so thick I didn't find it necessary to turn away or blush. "I need to see your knife," he said. He licked the blade, smacked his lips as though he could taste something. "Ohio?" he said.

"No, sir. Indiana."

"I don't know of any Indianans that can kill."

"I saw it with my own eyes," Father said. "Swear to god."

"Have you ever been to Indiana?" I said.

"Of course not."

"I lived there my whole life until today."

"It says something that you made it out. The trap is that you can see clear across to the other side but never actually reach it. How did you do it?"

"I'm a man," I said.

The woodsman pulled a bottle of moonshine from his chest hair. "Stakes," he said.

Father shrugged, handed me the bottle. I took one sniff and was ashamed. I pushed the bottle away. The woodsman struck me across the face. I stiffened my lips to keep from crying. Then he struck me again. I looked to Father for saving. "Kill him," Father said.

The woodsman was off and running, giggling like a maniac. I took a deep breath and steadied my emotions. I threw the knife. It landed upright in the grass after grazing the woodsman's genitals. The woodsman let out a terrific moan. Father swigged the moonshine. The woodsman gave me back the knife. He took off running again. I let the knife fall to my feet. "No more," I screamed, but I was too late. The woodsman ran headfirst into the pile of logs, splitting his skull wide open. The insides of his head seeped into the dirt.

I had dirt on my hands. "I think you should say something," I said to Father.

"He sure is dead," he said. He vomited next to the body. He asked for my sweater. He wiped his mouth clean, then covered the woodsman's face. When he noticed the stitches across my stomach, he told me to plead self-defense, whether it was god or the law that asked. I followed him into the woodsman's cabin, which he broke into by picking the lock with a crucifix. The woodsman had been living modestly. There was no furniture. Just more logs. Father went around opening all the doors. There were planks and woodchips and whittled sticks and not much else. He got down on his knees and scanned the floors for coins. I found a drawer full of miniature replicas of various trees, each tagged with a handwritten, cursive label: *pawpaw*, *alder*, *sumac*, *buckthorn*, etc. I thought they were beautiful. I told Father to look. He took a handful and threw them against the wall. I fit the rest of them in my pockets.

"This is all he had," Father said. "This is it."

"Roots," I said.

"Roots won't get you anywhere but buried in the dirt."

I didn't want to believe it. I looked out at the woodsman's lonesome body in the clearing. I turned back to Father to ask for help with burying, but he was gone. I dragged the body into the thicket myself.

My Mother Took to Keeping Tigers

THE BACKYARD BECAME AN ENCLOSURE. I couldn't sleep in my own bed. There were too many eyes—tigers' eyes—looking at me like I didn't belong. I went to her bedroom. She wasn't there. She was outside sleeping with the tigers. She lay on her back looking up at their bellies like skies full of stars. I told her I was scared. I pressed against the enclosure. My mother warned me not to get too close. "You can't touch everything you want," she said.

In the morning, my father appeared out of nowhere. I screamed, "I missed you," and he screamed, "Tigers." He locked us in the house. This time it was my mother who was gone. She let the tigers loose before she left. They paced the sidewalks, yawning. The SWAT team surrounded them. There is no mercy in the heartland. Or easy. Or escaping. All the tigers were dead. I had always thought their stripes looked like shattered glass, but now, with their carcasses splayed in the streets, they looked like lines on a map. I touched them, tracing each stripe in every direction. I felt for any signs of breath and blood pumping. I felt for any place else but here.

Postwar: Heartland

1.

THE SNIPER LEAVES HIS WIFE TO SAVE THE WHALES. No. That isn't true. The whales are a cover thought up by his wife, Sister. Actually, the sniper suffocated himself with a plastic grocery bag. And now Mother is expected at any moment. Suicide is a *no go*.

"Do you think whales are big enough?" Sister says to Brother. "Do you believe me?"

Sister and Brother are in the bedroom. The sniper's body is still on the bed.

Brother goes to the gun safe. "Where do you keep the bullets?"

"Not you too."

Brother flip-cocks an empty rifle. "I mean—it's so much easier."

"He was a professional. This wasn't about business."

"Was it about you?"

The doorbell rings. Mother is praying on the stoop. Brother helps her up from her knees.

"Where's your husband?" Mother says.

Brother nods at Sister like *go ahead*. Sister nods back like *I can't*. "After god's own heart," Brother finally says.

"Amen," Mother says.

"My husband," Sister says.

"Whales."

"Jonah?"

"He left me."

"To save them."

"Whales?"

"Endangered."

"Pollution."

"How long?"

"Long-term."

"Oceans apart."

"Divorce?"

"You'd never allow it—god wouldn't—"

"The great divorce," Brother says. "Of an entire species."

Sister falls into Mother's arms. Mother lifts a rosary out of her bosom. The crucifix hangs from her fingers over Sister's mouth. "I will pray for sharks," Mother says.

2.

Slugger is late for the ball game. Old Ball Coach is waiting for him in the dugout. "Fifth inning," he says.

"My father's gone," Slugger says.

"So's our lead." Old Ball Coach gives Slugger an aluminum bat. There's a runner on first. No men down. Old Ball Coach drags his index finger across his neck. Slugger misses on two attempts to sacrifice himself. Old Ball Coach walks up to Slugger, spits on him. "You're as good as buried now," he says.

Slugger digs in at the plate. His prayer is simple: *go far.*

He swings at the next pitch. Contact. A rope up the middle. The ball strikes the pitcher in the head. Slugger rounds first. Slugger rounds second and third. The game is called before Slugger is safe at home. There is a man down.

"If you knew the fundamentals," Old Ball Coach says.

"I was playing hurt," Slugger says.

"Heartache isn't real hurt."

"I miss him."

Old Ball Coach pulls the wad of dip from his lips. He rubs the dip over Slugger's heart. "If this don't make it better nothing will." Old Ball Coach removes his cap. "Maybe this don't seem like the right time," he says. "But what's right is right."

"Coach?"

"We're making a change."

"I can be better."

"It isn't about being better. It's about doing right by the game."

"I've been practicing."

"With who?"

"My father—"

Old Ball Coach puts his arm around Slugger. "I was your age once."

Slugger pushes Old Ball Coach away. "What do you know?"

"I don't know anything. I just make decisions." Old Ball Coach gives Slugger an envelope. "You would do the same in my position," he says.

"Japan?"

"It's a different game over there. You might stand a fighting chance."

"What about my family? My mother?"

Old Ball Coach's eyes well up with tears. The tears make trails in the dirt on his old leather face. He caresses the seam of a ball. "The hide is what's beautiful," he says. "Isn't it?"

3.

The plot is fucked. Flames shoot from the hole in the dirt. Brother covers his face. A sharp-toothed man, reeking of Oud Wood cologne, walks up behind him, puts his hands on Brother's hips. "Do you smell that?" the sharp-toothed man whispers in his ear.

"Yeah," Brother says, his eyes watering.

The sharp-toothed man takes the shovel from Brother, checks the coif of his hair in the blade. "This here gas field is worth millions. I'll give you a thousand. Cash."

"I can't."

"Is that your body?"

"My brother-in-law's."

"Dead, looks like."

"Yeah. And that's the plot."

"Is he somebody someone might come looking for?"

"No. He's a marine veteran."

The sharp-toothed man helps Brother drag the sniper's body to the flames. The body phoenixes.

"Now about the land," the sharp-toothed man says.

"It isn't mine."

"Then it's settled." The sharp-toothed man gives Brother a thousand-dollar bill. A construction crew erects a drill rig. The drill plunges into the earth.

"It's too big. My sister won't allow it."

"Do you believe in god?"

"I should."

"If this here was god, you'd say, 'Amen.' You'd say, 'Hallelujah.'"

"But I don't think god—"

"No. Don't *think* god. *Believe* him."

4.

Sister is crying over the eviction notice. "You said you'd give the money back."

"It only bought us a week."

An earthquake strikes the home. The ceiling splits. Mother falls through the crack and onto the sofa next to Sister. "Have you tried prayer?" Mother says.

"It won't work."

"You have to be born again, is all." Mother runs upstairs to the bathroom. She falls through the crack again. She leaps off the sofa. She fills up the kitchen sink.

"We can't drink the water," Brother says.

"Don't drink," Mother says. "Instead, let it fill you." She drags Sister by the hair, plunges her head into the water. When Sister is drowned, Mother turns to Brother. Brother backs away. Another earthquake. Much stronger. A ceiling beam dislodges. "Oh god," Mother says. And she is right. She is struck dead by the ceiling beam.

"This seems like a bad time," the sharp-toothed man says from outside an open window.

"We're all a little shaken up," Brother says.

"Well we've sprung a leak out here. I see you've got a swing set. Kids, maybe. But I can spare only one gas mask."

"He is out playing ball."

"I am still a good man," the sharp-toothed man says, tearing the rosary from around Mother's neck.

5.

Slugger is climbing Mount Kaikoma of Yamanashi Prefecture to retrieve a ball. He is 2,000 meters up and losing consciousness. He digs his spikes into the rock. He lifts himself onto a ridge where he rests, stiffening from the cold.

A serow appears before him, wearing the beard of god. Slugger's instincts stir in his stomach. He attempts to spike the throat of the serow. The serow leaps out of harm's way, shakes its beard of god at Slugger. "Americans," the serow bellows.

Valley fog engulfs the ridge. When it has passed, the serow is dead at Slugger's feet. The sniper drops his rifle. "But you're gone," Slugger says.

"We are all gone," the sniper says. He skins the serow and wraps its hide around Slugger. He holds him close until he stops shivering.

Slugger points to the summit of the mountain. "Did you find anything up there?"

"There is nothing up there. Absolutely nothing."

"Where are you going?"

"I'm sorry," the sniper says, leaping off the ridge.

6.

Sister is dead in the sniper's arms.

"There's only one mask," Brother says. "You understand?"

The sharp-toothed man pours gasoline around the house, drops a match. The house ignites.

Brother pulls off the gas mask and plunges his head into the sink.

The sharp-toothed man knocks on the front door. The front door turns to ash.

The drill continues through the earth. Fucks it. Fucks it.

The sharp-toothed man unbuttons his shirt, wipes the sweat off his face. "Who are you and why are you still here?" he says.

The sniper spits, hitting the sharp-toothed man between the eyes.

The sharp-toothed man grins. Earlier, he swallowed Mother's crucifix. It glows like another, sharper tooth in the back of his throat. He thumbs through a bible that he found at his feet. It feels heavy to him, at first. And then it feels like nothing. Whole verses evaporate. The cover melts, like tar seeping between his fingers. "Exodus," he repeats. "Exodus. Exodus."

I Am the Heaviest Feeling Man on the Planet

THE TV DECIDES FOR HIM THAT HE SHOULD HAVE EVERYTHING. And then suddenly there he is, crashed through the glass front of a fast-casual American restaurant, concussed, and bleeding from the nose. He's fallen into a ball pit. The balls stick to his clothes. He removes his clothes. He can't remove his skin. He feels them like overgrown pustules. The small hand of a boy smelling like the lake reaches in, pulls him out.

•

The man opens his mouth to speak. The boy speaks for him: "Who are you?" And the boy says back, "I know what all that you want." He slices a sandwich bun in half, arranges the two halves outside so that the entire premises is between them. He goes to the cash register, rings the order up, screams, "Everything!" Loud, manic typing. The receipt is several feet long, covered in ellipses. "Are you sure?" the boy says. The man crumples the receipt into a ball, swallows it.

•

He consumes the stores of meat, sides, condiments, and cooking grease, sucks soda syrup from what looks like blood bags, sniffs the salt, pepper, and red pepper flakes. He points to the boy, opens his mouth. "Turn the TVs on," the boy speaks for him. The TVs scream at each other.

•

The TVs are screaming at him. "I am the heaviest feeling man on the planet," the boy speaks for him. The man sobs over a stack of napkins, which he then consumes in soggy wedges like pancakes, along with the rest of the paperware, plasticware, and cleaning products.

•

And the dirt on the floor and the little bugs in the corners and in the cupboards and the undersides of the shelves and the fruit flies and their nests in the drains and the drain clog remover and the insulation in the walls and the doorknobs and the doors and the window and the blood in his mouth after eating all that glass and the ball-pit balls after a good rinsing and then the rinse water, the toilet water, the puddle of condensation next to the walk-in freezer.

•

And a napkin with a note written in lipstick: *We'll discuss this when we get home.*

•

And then a hush falls over the restaurant. The TVs display a waving flag, screens buzzing. A burst of horns. The man and the boy stand up, their hands over each other's hearts. It is a commercial for something, though they miss what for, too busy wiping their welled-up eyes.

•

And wiping the snot from their noses with their hands and then the man licks his hands and the boy's hands clean and the TVs are screaming again.

•

The boy is holding a very large fish across his chest. He asks, "When's the last time you went fishing?"

"Yes," the boy speaks for the man. "When. I don't like pinching the worms in half with my fingers when they're still alive."

•

The fish is dead. The man kneels before the dead fish, salivating.

•

Several flashes of light.

•

A crowd is gathered outside. Passersby, reporters, photographers. A woman on a gurney covered in a sheet. "Who is she?" the boy speaks for the man. The boy says nothing back.

•

The fish is empty on the inside, lying on the floor, stinking.

•

The boy says he is going out for a smoke and is gone.

•

One of the reporters asks the man to say something. He just opens his mouth. And another reporter breaches the sandwich buns, puts a camera too close to the man's face. The man bites his ear off, then into the reporter's neck until it sprays blood all over the crowd. They disperse, screaming.

•

The man is on the TVs baring his teeth, covered in blood. The crawl says: *Breaking.*

•

The woman on the gurney is next to him. She lifts the sheet off her body with her teeth. There is no body. She is a head, is all. She tells the man to finish what she couldn't. She says, "Finish me." And the man says:

•

And the woman says, "Look! There!" She points to the TVs with her tongue. The flag. The horns. The man consumes the TVs. His insides crackle, pop. Smoke coming out of his ears.

•

And the Burger King is there too. He holds the woman in his hands. "Where has your gambol gone?" he says and he laughs and she laughs.

•

And the man takes the ® hovering over the Burger King's left shoulder and eats it.

•

And the boy is there again.

"The fishmonger!" the Burger King rages, dropping the woman to the ground.

•

The Burger King lunges for the boy. The boy leaps out of reach and onto the woman's gurney. He fashions the sheet into a sail and is off! The man opens his mouth. The boy speaks for him, "The bun! The bun!" The boy is waving one of the halves in the air. The man tries to chase after him but is too full to keep up. The distance between them grows wider. Everything needing to be consumed becomes even more.

Love to a Monster

The woman said, "Lie back. Show me your teeth." She was speaking to the wolf. The man watched them through a crack in the bedroom door. They tumbled onto the bed. They tore the sheets, each other's skin, sex in the air like confetti.

"Deeper," she told the wolf.

They finished each other.

"I taste blood," the wolf said.

"Me too," the woman said.

The man pushed the door open.

The wolf leaped into the closet.

"How could you?" the woman said to the man.

"I'm not mad," the man said.

"Of course not. That's the problem." She leaped out the open window.

The wolf lay in the closet, bleeding. "I've made a mess of your home."

The man took a needle and thread and made a suture of the wolf's wound. Then he asked the wolf to leave.

"But I'm afraid," the wolf said.

"I'm the one who should be afraid," the man said. He was right. The wolf swallowed him whole. The man howled from inside the wolf until the police showed, then animal control, then tranquilizers, a cage.

He woke up on a floor covered with newspaper. The animal warden forced his muzzle open and fed him a bone.

"But I'm not an animal," he yelped.

The animal warden loaded a gun. "Then you must be a monster. If I weren't so humane, I'd drown you in the river like the others."

He shut his eyes, waiting for the bullet. Instead, he felt the woman's hands around his throat.

"My wolf," she said.

"My woman," he said.

It was spring. They walked through a field of flowers together. He pissed on a tree and asked the woman if she still loved him. The woman kissed his teeth with her teeth. She ran her fingers through his fur. She found the suture. She tore it open like a seam, pulling the wolf's skin off the man. "You're a monster," she screamed.

"No. Look at my teeth."

"I didn't come for you."

The man pulled a dandelion from the dirt, twisted its stem into a ring. He slipped it onto the woman's finger. She struck him in the face with the dandelion ring. A dandelion grew from the wound. The man pulled it out. Another grew in its place, then another and another until his skin was all dandelions. The woman sneezed. The dandelions burst.

"Have you ever made love to a monster?" he said.

The woman kept sneezing.

When he reached to pull her closer, he caught a fistful of dandelion seeds. They stuck out from between his fingers like eyes in the dark of an open door.

"Do you feel them watching?" he said.

"I feel them," she said. And then she said, "And nothing."

A Black Eye. A Drowned Eye.

It begins with a sore throat. Some trouble swallowing. An abscess.

Then an enormous bloodshot eye growing out of the abscess and overtaking the rest of her.

She is very peculiar!

Her husband is furious that he can't understand what she is looking for.

Though the pupil widens like a mouth, she can't scream.

She rolls into the sea.

At the bottom of the sea she meets a fish.

"What are you looking at?" the fish says.

She is looking at the hook protruding from the fish's throat.

"This isn't what it feels like," the fish says.

But it is. She is caught in a fishnet. She is flailing on the deck of a fishing boat. She is set raw on a dinner plate, looking up at the cyclops.

"It says here you are very peculiar," the cyclops says, holding this story in front of her.

She begins at *It begins...*

Everything is exactly how it happened except for the fish? Where is the fish?

The cyclops drinks a glass of water.

At the bottom of the glass is an enormous eye, badly swollen and blue.

A black eye. A drowned eye.

She would like to knock on the glass at the eye.

She is heartsick for her vanished hands.

She wants out like a fish inside a fish tank but with hands, knocking and clawing.

The cyclops has her pinned to the plate with the fork.

The knife is somewhere close. The hook is inside her still.

She was always the fish.

Two Brothers Cut from Stars

Two brothers, Bull and Whip, hold unsteady the thwart of a boat in the rough waters of a great lake. Bull leans over the hull and vomits. The vomit dissolves in the water. He presses his hands into the water, but they do not dissolve. They ache. He has splinters from when he feared letting go, from when Whip forced him to let go, prying his fingers from the bulkhead, demanding he help row. Bull will row no more. Bull says, "I'm sick of the water." Whip throws Bull onto the bottom boards. Bull says, "I don't hurt."

Whip kneels beside Bull, says, "Brother."

"Where are we?"

"We can't know for sure until we can see Polaris."

It has been three days in the boat on the lake, and now the boat is filling up with water. Bull thinks it must be the bottoms of their feet, how rough they got going up the mountain. Whip asks how deep it has become. Bull says he can't swim. They are sinking. The lake wraps around their necks. They reach for each other. They reach for fish, for anything. Night falls on them like a shot canvasback.

They are all that is left after their mother had the aneurysm and their father used a shotgun on himself the same evening. The brothers buried them together in a hole they dug in the backyard. They rinsed the dirt off their hands and faces with the hose, drank from the hose. They lay on the grave until the morning.

Bull said, "I still smell the blood." He let the hose run until the grave turned to mud. He fell into the mud. The more he struggled, the deeper he sank. Whip pulled and pulled. Bull went deeper and deeper. He was sobbing.

"It's okay. You aren't dead."

"But I'm touching them."

THEY LEFT for anywhere else. Whip led because he could kill. They made it to the mountain when Bull said, "We can turn back."

Whip said, "To what?"

"Home."

"It's just us now. There's no home."

They struggled up the mountain. They were barefoot, their shoes shredded by the rock surface. It was cold. Dark. Whip disappeared into the brush to gather wood for fire. Bull ripped the dead skin off his hands and feet. Then he screamed, "I see light."

"Where?"

"The valley."

Whip pulled out his spyglass. "An old cabin."

"It means we aren't dead."

"We aren't dead."

"Do you think they see us?"

"Who?"

"The family in the cabin."

"It's just stones here and the cold."

"And us?"

"Just us."

BULL IS thinking death underwater when Whip yells, "Rope."

They are pulled to shore. Bull collapses onto the sand. Whip shakes dry. He blushes when he sees her. She is wearing a sequin dress. She says, "My hair."

Whip says, "My brother."

Bull can't breathe. The sequin girl presses her lips onto his and sucks the water out of his lungs like smoke. Her eyes fill with water. She coughs. Whip presses his lips onto hers until she says, "We are all not dead." The brothers are still tied up in her hair. Whip untangles them and helps her wrap it into a tight spool.

WHIP SAID it was fate as he loosened the abandoned boat from the pier. Bull was shaken from being unable to see across the water to land. They rowed toward the sun. When the sun set they rowed toward the stars. Bull could see the fish speaking, but couldn't hear them through the water. Whip jumped in and tried to catch one with his hands. Bull said, "Who taught you to swim?"

Whip said, "I did. I learned with floats."

"What floats?"

"I filled my pockets with corks. When I got good, I took off my pants."

"Bullshit."

"We all learn with floats. As long as there are people, there will be floats. Same as anything else. Same as hats, even. There'll always be hats because of heads. And if even we lose our heads, if we turn into headless things, there'll still be hats. We'll wear them where our heads were. The nub of our necks. I bet you we call them hats heads. We'll wear hats on the hats we call heads. I think about it sometimes when no one's looking." Whip takes Bull's hand, tries to pull him into the water.

Bull strikes the water, rages against the water, scaring all the fish away. He sobs. "How much longer?"

And Whip says, "It isn't an ocean."

"Does that mean soon?"

BULL COMPLAINS that they haven't eaten. The sequin girl notices the heaviness in his movements, takes him to a flat stone, lays him down, says, "Sleep." She covers him with her hair. Bull feels overcome with weightlessness, adrift in the sequins; her body the moon, and he is out there somewhere he can't explain.

Whip says, "It's all shit," as he combs the beach with his fingers, searching.

Bull is cold suddenly. The sequin girl feels him shiver. She says, "Are you the baby?" She wraps him tighter. Bull tries to shake her lose. She goes, "Baby, baby, baby." He closes his eyes, thinking she may vanish then. She begins a lullaby. Whip interrupts to say he has found a hook. He crawls to Bull to show him the hook. He pierces his own skin with the hook. Bull touches Whip's wound, tells him it is a good hook. Whip says it isn't enough. He sharpens it against the stone. Sparks. He threads the hook with a strand of the sequin girl's hair. He casts the line into the lake. Bull casts his eyes on the stars.

THE THUD of their mother's body turned everything quiet. They found her on the porch, lay next to her body until their father came home. He said, "Boys," stepping over them. Later, he tucked them into bed and said, "Remember, there's just you." Then his blood covered the balcony and his body and her body. The brothers dragged them to the backyard and unsettled the dirt. Bull asked if this was what was meant by love and Whip said, "Maybe."

WHIP SAYS, "I got one." He holds the wriggling fish in his shirt like a bassinet. The sequin girl builds a fire. She breathes into it and it grows. Whip carries the fish to the fire. He asks Bull for a stone. Bull says, "I can do it."

Whip says, "No. Let her."

The sequin girl lifts the stone high over her head. Whip straddles the fish to keep it from moving. The sequin girl brings the stone down onto the fish's head, but the fish doesn't die.

Bull says, "I told you."

The sequin girl and Whip switch positions. The fish quivers between her thighs. Whip takes the hook, latches it to the cord at the base of the fish's throat, the tendon between the gills, and rips it apart. He bends the fish's head back until it snaps off the spine. The fish squirts all over the sequin girl's dress. She sets it by the fire to dry. Whip tears the fish open. Roasts it. The fish's bones crackle. When it's finished, Whip and the sequin girl tear the meat off the fish's bones with their teeth. Bull says, "We need to keep moving." Whip gives him the caudal fin. Bull fingers the fin, draws blood.

THE FIRE is dead. Whip and the sequin girl lie entangled. Morning. The sequin girl washes her hair in the water. Whip calls for Bull. No answer. The swooshing of water. The breeze. Whip calls out, "Bull."

The sequin girl says, "There's nowhere else. You can't escape this. Yonder it's just thicket."

Whip tries to see through the trees with his spyglass. The sequin girl takes it in her hands, buries it in the sand. She says, "And nothing."

Whip says, "We're brothers."

"He'll come back."

He is lost in the thicket. The trees are sapping heavily. He tastes it until his teeth ache, his stomach hurts. He tries to push through the trees but can't. So he goes up. Climbs. He stabs the caudal fin into the trunk, carves his way up to the top. He feels weightlessness again, looking out into the vastness, wanting to touch so much that he can't. The sun goes *goodbye*. Polaris goes *this way*. And the dippers go *you can only have what you can hold.*

Animals

It's been three months of K. not sleeping, of K. not coming to bed, even. I lie alone like the Vitruvian Man. She paces the living room watching the television.

"Everything feels like one day," she says. "And this one day just won't end."

I say, "What did you do today?"

"I sat in the bathroom with my face against the tiles."

"Did it make you feel better?"

"The bathroom is very clean."

"I try."

"When I was young, the bathroom was always dirty. It smells like an island now."

I purchased that scented plug-in because we've never had a honeymoon. "You choose the next scent," I say. "Any place you want."

"I'm old," she says.

"It isn't true. If you're old, I'm old. Look at me and be honest."

"You left the stove on this morning. I smelled gas all day."

"I still smell it."

"I hoped it would put me to sleep."

"This isn't working."

"Should I light a match?"

"What do you want me to do?"

"*You're* the inventor."

"Inventory analysis," I say.

And K. says, "What does it mean when I look at my fingers and all I can think of is multiplication?" She shows me her hands. I ask her to make fists. She sobs. "Paws," she says. "They look like paws." I take them into my hands. I tell her I will do everything I can for her. I shut the stove off. I open all the windows. I set out on my promise of everything.

I'm finished in two days. I whisper in K.'s ear, "Look up," and she screams. I have constructed a mobile out of animals I caught in our backyard. They hang from wires tied to the blades of the ceiling fan above our bed. "They aren't dead," I say. "I used cough syrup."

"One of them is empty."

"Look closer."

"An ant?"

After securing the groundhog, squirrel, rabbit, and chipmunk, it was the best I could do. Deer are too heavy, children too loud and too cared for.

"It's still moving. It wants free."

"I didn't know how much to give it. But look how relaxed the rest of them look!" I set the fan on its slowest setting. I turn the key to a music box I found in the attic with our old things. I take K. to bed. "Look," I say, as the animals pass over us like slouching angels. I can't keep my eyes open any longer. "Baby," I say. "Are you still awake?" I don't get an answer because I'm not. In the morning, I discover the wires have been cut. The animals are gone.

Postwar: Apiary, Aviary

I WASHED DISHES AT A RESTAURANT I COULDN'T AFFORD TO EAT AT. I was outside on a smoke break when a woman approached me and complained about the knives being dull. I told her it was out of my hands. She took my hands.

My knuckles were fucked from the speed bag I had rigged from the ceiling in my apartment. I got fucked when I tried to keep up with the neighbors upstairs. They had lasted longer than I was ready for.

I had been swollen for days.

I head my cigarette between fingertips. I got signed, flinched. "I didn't mean to hurt you," she said.

I was an amateur.

I WANTED to fight a man called Roderick who went by Ron because he had war stories and what did I have? I was all instinct and fists up. "Come on."

He was talking about a boy found in the jungle rotted to bones wearing dog tags marked CATHOLIC. Bees made a hive of his skull. The soldiers gave up their John Wayne bars for honey. It was tough to swallow. "If you're set on hitting me," he said, "Do me one better." He took out his combat knife. He set it at my feet. "I serrated this blade myself when I was young like you and scared."

I DIDN'T know where I was going. I had exhausted my connections, ending up on the number six bus at 4 a.m. headed south out of the city. It was me and this other guy who lay on his back over two seats, his eyes swollen shut. I asked him if he fought.

"I don't have nothing else," he said. He crawled off at the last stop within city limits.

The driver had his eyes on me. "Missed my stop," I said.

"Where to?"

"I'd like to go back."

"You'll have to wait."

We pulled into the dark of the maintenance yard where out-of-service railcars and bus chassis lay scattered like postwar. The driver hosed down the aisle. I watched the grime slide out the doors.

I HAD in my head wants, and the want I thought simplest and least full of hurt was to hurt. I practiced hurting the speed bag and the pillows and the mattress I had set up against the wall. I slept on the hardwood floor. I wanted to be a man like I was supposed to.

That was as far as I could take it. That was all I had.

And that's what I told the man who tried to mug me at the bus stop. It could have been a gun in his coat pocket. That could have been it and that's what I was thinking about: it and what it means. He patted me down. He found the combat knife. "Why didn't you try to fight back?" he said.

"FORGET THE knives," the woman said. "Forget I ever said anything."

"I was going to let someone know."

"I want it like it never happened."

"Isn't anything I'm ashamed of."

"Do you drink?"

I drove her Buick through the suburbs and the sprawl. The flat and straight of the road allowed my hands rest. I counted the cracks in the skin of the swelling like tick marks on the scale of a map.

It was about direction.

She demanded that I look at her.

I WAS feeling at home where I shouldn't have, counting the threads in the bedsheets. I went for my cigarettes like an old film. "You can't do that here," she said.

I WAS ready to fight when he emerged from behind a bee box in the backyard. "They're only threats if you are," he said. "You my wife's?" He removed the top of the bee box. He held up the shallow chamber. "Smoke keeps them calm."

Neither of us were protected. They crawled over his fingers and his wrists. They landed on my shoulders and my neck. I stood tough and still as I could. I blew smoke slow through my nostrils. I was the bull.

"We have an aviary too," he said.

THERE WERE no birds in the aviary. It was just a small garden and a wooden rocket ship.

"Is there anything you would miss?" he said.

"I don't know."

"I also thought I didn't know."

I touched a nylon cord that hung from the fins. "Ignition?"

"I had it planned that way some moons ago."

ANOTHER MOON. I climbed into the rocket ship with no one knowing I was still around. I spent the night with the nylon cord in my lap. My fists stung. My head buzzed. I'm not saying I had expected lift off. I'm saying just that it wasn't.

Snuff Film

THE MAN LAUNCHES A ROCKET FROM THE BACKYARD. The woman's face is hot with exhaust. The rocket approaches the stratosphere. White noise. A priest riding past on a motorcycle, displaying a low hand gesture, then loosening his collar. He sees the rocket. Stops. He snaps a photo of the rocket with a Polaroid camera. The photo develops with a burn in the middle where the thrusters should be. At the same time some neighborhood boys are shooting a snuff film with a Super 8. They've already offed a dog on the side of the road with a jerrican of gasoline and matches, and then a bag of dogs with a body of water. The boys sneak up on the priest. They point their cameras at each other. The world buckles. The man never removed the chain. The world is tethered to the rocket, hurtling through the universe. The sun becomes very small, then is gone. There are no more days, just a continuousness. An apocalypse with no end: the untimes. There is no gravity. It is either hold on or let go. "Tell me what," the woman says to the man. Then she is going, going. The man reaches after her. She is too far beyond him. He turns to the boys. The boys don't look back. They are watching a pack of dogs, also floating up and away, together.

Commuter

I REEMERGED FIFTEEN YEARS LATER. I wasn't supposed to come back. "Miraculous," I guffawed in front of the man I presumed a coworker, the man attempting to conceal that he had been masturbating at his desk, our desk.

I was thinking about my wife. "Are you married?" I said.

"Who isn't," he said.

Simultaneous to my elation, I was worried about the possible dangers associated with a reemergence, something akin to explosive decompression. I checked myself for missing or malformed appendages. "I am wholly here," I said, relieved. My coworker stuffed the lubricant and Kleenex into a drawer, zipped up his pants, and huffed off deflated in a way I was grateful that I wasn't. I opened the drawer, considered what was at my disposal. I studied the palms of my hands. Lifelines. I had lived a life, and I was living again. As for the in-between, nobody had been sure back then. The idea was what if there was a better morally acceptable form of suicide, what if a suicide could be, simply, strategic disappearance, like being set aside for safekeeping in a lockbox until nature ran its course and snuffed us out the regular way. I had been told to think of it like a pause, like a very long commute.

On my way out of the office the night guard asked if I had attained any sort of enlightenment, if the world seemed different to me spiritually, if there was a god, if I had met god, what was he like, god, was he he, she, or it? "Is this it?" the night guard said.

There was some enlightenment. When I came home the first time since reemerging, I found another man on the porch. I felt violent. I held back. I asked what time it was. What year. But all he said was that he was sorry, that all he knew was that it was a bad time for all of us now.

The night guard asked if I had attained a longer, wider view of the world, was what's important in life what is in front of us, behind us, or beyond us? What was beyond us? Did I go to sleep thinking about yesterday or tomorrow? Did I ever get caught up thinking about everyone that had come before me, will come after me? "If I was you, I wouldn't want a list of everyone who had died when I was gone," the night guard said. "Or else I'd spend the rest of my life saying goodbye."

I wasn't ready to go home. I went back to the office, slept at my desk.

"How will you explain it to the ones you love?" the night guard said. "Is it love or are you just a stranger now?"

"No. I am a commuter."

The night guard asked if it was all preordained, that if I lived to be a thousand years old, would I have even the slightest understanding of the world? "And would you believe I almost became a minister?" He gave me a pocket-sized bible, said it would help with my reacclimatization.

I woke up in a conference room, surrounded by my coworkers and the supervisor. He snatched the bible away, handed me the standard operating procedure. He had highlighted the most pertinent section: no one was supposed to come back. I wasn't supposed to be here. Someone asked if I should be killed. A hush fell over the room. They asked if killing was in the revised SOP. If killing counted as a workplace injury. If killing came with overtime pay. They began to chant, "Kill him." But we all looked so similar, frightened and tired. They started in on each other. No one noticed I had snuck out of the room. I wondered how many of them ended up dead.

"What did they ever do to you?"

"Don't you mean: what did they do to me?"

I asked the kid how he would have answered that. We were standing in the park at the end of the street. I couldn't go home still. The kid pointed up a tree. He said there had been monsters in that tree, that he killed them all, the monsters.

"Monsters?" I said.

"Not anymore," he said.

"Because you killed them."

"I wanted to hurt them at first."

"Isn't that the same thing?"

"I hope not."

"Would you believe me if I said we used to be happy?" I said to the man on my porch.

"We used to be happy too," he said.

"I don't blame you."

"I blame myself. I was somewhere else completely."

"She asked me what we were accomplishing together anymore."

"She said it was like we stopped growing together."

"She said I was always gone."

"I was gone. And here I am now."

We were searching the porch for the spare key. We checked the awnings, under the welcome mat, the cracks in the foundation. The front door was already unlocked.

"I'm just trying to understand," the night guard said.

"So am I," I said.

"Was it space? Did you want space?"

"I don't know."

"Were you dead?"

"I'm home," we said. There were more of us, too many of us. The floor was buckling under the weight.

"Stay back or I'll hurt you," the kid said. We studied him for resemblances. He was trying to protect her. She hadn't expected that we'd come back. And why should she?

"Did it feel like your last night on Earth? Was it palpable? The ending. Was it supposed to be an ending?"

"I don't know," I said.

"Help me," we said.

I Bought Her a Bird

I BOUGHT HER A BIRD FOR US, A LIFE THAT WE COULD BOTH TOUCH. I hold up the cage. "Look," I say. "It can't go anywhere."

And she says, "But I am," and then she's gone.

It's me and the bird and the cage. "Bird," I begin, but that's all I've got right now. It hops from hanging block of wood to hanging block of wood, pecking at its reflection in the miniature mirror. How cruel the wilderness must be! I try imagining a life without mirrors, life with other birds and things much bigger than other birds, predators, winter, exposure to the elements, the need to flee the changing of seasons. I am grateful for the miracle that is suburban Cleveland, Ohio. "Bird," I say. "You'll never need anywhere else again." The bird peeps. My wife has no idea what she's missing! When I try to pet its feathers, it pecks at my fingers. "I am not a worm!" I shout like the elephant man, and I think we're sharing a good laugh. I stay up late and watch the bird sleep.

"Where was I?" she says, kissing me awake the next morning.

"I don't know," I say.

"Nothing was what I expected, so I just kept going. That's where."

"Where?"

"I made it about halfway through Indiana when I realized I was overdressed."

The bird wakes up and sings its morning song.

She says, "You look how I feel."

"I'm just tired."

"Yeah."

"It was a wild night. Our bird can sing."

She's packing sweatpants into a suitcase. "I came for a change of clothes, is all."

"Don't you want to sleep?"

"I have to finish Indiana first."

Two days later, she bursts through the door and shouts, "Help me." There are hundreds of ears of corn on our porch. "This is the best I've ever seen," she says. "All it needs is shucked."

We pile it on the living room floor. I peel back a husk. I admit these are gorgeous. I drop the finest yellow kernel I can find in the birdcage. Then I try one myself. "Indiana's sweet," I say.

"No. This is from Illinois."

"Chicago?"

"Hoopeston."

"What happened to Indiana?"

"The Pizza King."

"The Pizza King?"

"I think he misheard me when I said I needed a meal. He said there's no meal quite like Illinois meal. He showed me his map and I touched it." She has locked herself in our bedroom. I knock. She says, "I'm changing." She opens the door. She's wearing a brightly colored sundress. She stands over the birdcage. "It's getting old," she says. "Isn't it?" She runs out of the house. I shout that she's forgotten her suitcase. "It's a hundred degrees in Missouruh," she says. "This is all I'll need."

"Missouri?"

"Missouruh. You have to say it right or else it'll be obvious to everyone you don't belong."

"Misery," I say, lifting the bird out of the cage. It pecks at me again, this time drawing blood. I let the bird go and it drops. I'm confused. I lift the bird again, let it go, and it drops. Hard. "You can't fly?" I say. I set the body back in the cage.

"Surprise!" she says. She is covered in snow.

"How long's it been?" I say.

She takes my hands in her cold hands, sets a heavy stone in my palm. "It's gold," she says. "The portions out West are huge. Ohio has been holding back our whole lives."

I fall asleep holding the gold in one hand and the dead bird in the other. I wake up struggling in a sea of casino chips. I can't swim. I reach for anything. There's no gold, no dead bird, and no her. There's a note: YOU ARE VERY LUCKY! At the bottom of the sea of casino chips, I find the dead bird. I take its wishbone. I feel her hands on me. She pulls me out. I can hardly recognize her anymore. Her hair is dyed blonde. Somebody drew a mole above her lips. She's wearing a gown we can't afford.

There's a knock at the door. In walks the Pizza King, big and broad-shouldered and gold-crowned and dressed in an expensive white suit. He hands me a handkerchief worth more than I could ever be worth. "This is for when you start crying," the Pizza King says. He wraps his arms around her.

"I might have a future in pictures," she says. "I might have a future."

"Have you ever seen anything more beautiful in your life?" the Pizza King says.

And then they are both gone.
And me? I haven't.

Heartland Wilds

I RETURNED HOME TO THE WILDS AND STRUCK PA AS HARD AS I WAS ABLE. It took him a long time to come to. I stood over him, bigger. I saw a lot of me beneath the swelling.

"Boy?"

"Square in the jaw."

"Missed."

My knuckles smarted. I flexed my hand to see whether any blood got loose. I palmed the wall to check that my fingers were still straight.

"I haven't eaten, is all," Pa said. "I'm not right for what I got coming for me."

"You got blood."

"All over."

I opened the cold box, the cupboards. All empty. "Ma deserves—" I began and Pa told me shush, motioning to the bedroom. It was empty also. "Where's she?"

"Quiet."

I struck him square in his pursed lips.

"She's done for," Pa said, solemn. "There's folks around here I don't want knowing."

I touched the indent of her shape in the bed.

Pa crawled to my feet, resting his swollen face on my thigh. "This isn't the last thing. We raised you to believe there's more."

"I don't believe you."

"You came back."

"Wasn't done for."

"Far as we could tell you were."

"Went for a walk."

"You're less same than you were when you left."

"Grew up."

"You saying you're a man?"

"I'm saying I hit you square and it hurt."

"Square's not shit. Can you fish, even?"

I reared back.

Pa put up his hands. "Course you can't. I never showed you." He pointed out the window. "Look at all them scales in the moonlight. Fetch my hooks, my worms."

WE SAT on the bank of the river. I sunk my feet into the water. "Wish I'd taught you better," Pa said, casting his line.

I remembered the old days when the wilds were thicker. When Ma stood at the window, watching over me as she readied supper. When Pa sat quietly in the yard with a pipe and a paper. I'd told him I'd like to fish for evening's supper and Pa said I could, shooing me away with the rolled-up paper. I did what he'd told me to do like I was supposed to. I'd gone and kept going until I ended up where I'd left.

Pa hooked a fish with no trouble, lifting it from the river. "Want you to have this," he said, setting the fish on my lap. "Remember: we weren't all bad." It was the last thing he said before jumping into the river.

I stuck the fish into the ice pail. I carried it to where the river was widest. I searched for Pa. I found a child instead.

"Bites?" the child said.

"I'm going to let it go."

"Smells done for."

"That's right."

I dumped out the ice pail. The fish broke apart in the river.

"I don't understand," the child said. "You could've fed your folks."

"No folks no more."

The child knelt before me and prayed.

I shoved him away. "No place for that."

"I'll tell Mother," the child sobbed.

"She's gone."

The child struck me in the knee and ran off.

I looked back down at the river. Nothing. I went home.

I FELL asleep inside the shape of Ma. I woke up and there were more children. I was surrounded. The child who'd struck me at the river climbed onto the bed, grabbed me by the hair.

"Him," the child shrieked to a woman who appeared suddenly next to the bed. She stared out the window, paying no attention to the child or what the child was saying.

I tried to sit up. The children pressed me down with their tiny hands.

"No more leaving," the woman said.

"I'm already here," I said. "Aren't I."

"This is home."

"I know."

The children cheered at this truth like it was an admission. They touched me softer. They tugged at me, embraced me.

"Shall we fish?" the woman asked.

The children squealed.

I smelled the fish. They were boiling in a pail on the stove.

The woman ladled the fish and the fish broth into bowls. I stared at the fish head set before me. It steamed into my face. When I reached for a spoon, the children gasped.

"We can't begin until we understand how this is possible," the woman said.

"Who?" the children said.

"Yes," the woman said. "Who?"

"Mother."

THE FISH head didn't sit well. I choked it up into the toilet.

"What do you see?" Mother said.

The fish head stared back at me.

"No," Mother said. "Look at me."

I couldn't. I choked up again: more bones, broth, and scales.

MOTHER WAS outside, forcing the children to dig. "For me," she repeated.

"We love you," the children said.

The child who'd struck me took my hand and brought me to the hole he'd begun. "I'm scared it's too shallow," he said. "If it's too shallow..." he trailed off. His hands were bloody and raw. I fetched the fish pail and helped him dig a little deeper.

Mother stood over us and said, "It's not enough. It's never enough."

"I know," I said. "I know."

The child climbed into the hole. "But I fit!"

"Stay down," Mother said.

I WENT to the river. I washed my head and hands. I watched the fish. And then I saw something that forced me to my feet. Before I could dive into the river, Mother had me in her grip and was dragging me back home. "You could've drowned," she screamed. Then she pulled a spade from between her breasts. "Here."

"Why?"

"There's so much you don't understand."

"You understand?"

"I'm trying." She climbed into a hole.

The children were already buried.

"I thought I saw Pa in the river," I said, looking down at her.

"Do you believe that?"

"I shouldn't."

"Would you believe me if I told you?"

I could still taste the fish head. And blood. I had little cuts in my tongue from the bones. "I don't know," I said.

"There's a lot we can't do on our own," she said. Maybe she was praying.

I filled the hole like she needed. I struck the dirt flush with the flats of my fists.

The Water Is the Last Thing

1. I WANTED IT TO END LIKE THIS:

2. I watched a woman give birth in the waiting room. Stillborn. *I want to name it* she screamed, as she was being wheeled away empty-handed; the heavy, swinging doors to the operating room whooshing shut behind her.

3. The television had war on loop. An exit-sign light went out. Worried people dug into their pockets for cigarettes, watching the clocks on the wall, trying to figure out how many they could finish before whatever they were waiting on happened.

4. A man wearing an Elizabethan collar slumped over the receptionist desk. He clutched his chest with both hands. He had no other credentials. *It's my heart* he said. He unbuttoned his shirt. *Look at it. My heart*

5. Somebody called a code blue over the loudspeaker. It was an emergency. We all were.

6. I stepped over the body of a man who lay fetal on the floor. *The bullet isn't fatal* another wounded man said, possibly the shooter. *But the infection will be.* He turned to the nurse. *Tell him*

it's curtains he said. *Tell him the curtains are dirty.* Everyone shared a good, hearty laugh.

7. I found temporary quiet inside a bathroom stall. I bled into the toilet. I bled into the sink. I heard my name called.

8. The receptionist was seated high up like an altar. *I'm sorry I made a mess* I said. *Yes* she said. *But the floor is vitrified* she said. She offered me a mop. She asked me my occupation. I told her it had been an accident. She demanded that I answer her questions truthfully. *We don't want mistakes* she said. *But it was* I said.

9. I was having trouble writing on the forms she gave me. *Is there someone close to you that can help you?* she said. *No* I said. *Nobody?* she said. *Do you think that might be a symptom or a cause?*

10. An orderly pressed me onto a gurney. A nurse pressed down on the big vein in my neck. *I'll make it* I said. I don't know why. *You hope so* the nurse said. Did she know? A doctor opened her white coat. *Here are my needles* she said. *You choose.* I chose. She pushed it through my ribs. *Tell me how bad it feels* she said. *I don't feel anything* I said. *Good good* she said.

11. *Good good* the doctor repeated when I woke some hours later. My left arm was gone. *Wait* I said. *Why should I?* she said. And she didn't.

12. *Is there someone we can call?* the nurse said. *A Taxi* I said.

13. Thin walls. I heard every spasm and obstructed artery and gap in breathing. I stared at the food tray. The utensils looked difficult. I saw myself in the bend of the spoon. I saw also the

fluorescent lights in the ceiling, the buzzing and the heat. I thought of a magnifying glass and an insect.

14. *Are you awake?* the nurse said. She opened the curtain around my bed. *I think so* I said. *Good* she said. *You'll be released first thing in the morning. We found someone.* She shut the curtain. *You don't have to go* I said, imagining her sitting bedside as I slept, my cut off arm in her arms. *No* she said. *But you do*

15. The orderly again. *I thought it was over* I said. *Good doctor* the orderly said. We followed the nurse through the corridors. Crucifix-sharp turns. *I wanted it* I began. The orderly squeezed my shoulders. Then a bright yellow light. *Are you afraid?* he said. *Are you afraid?* the nurse said. She IVed me calm before I could answer.

16. I came to in a chair in the captain's office. He was tapping at a calculator. My X-rays were taped to a window. *Do you understand the cost?* he said. He swiveled in his big chair. He pointed to the X-rays. *It was an accident* I said.

17. The captain had been in the navy. He still wore the hat and the peacoat, his pants cuffed like he was standing in high waters. He had anchors tattooed on his calves. *It's just an excuse* he said.

18. The office walls were painted blue. There were photos of the bodies of water he had navigated. A stuffed marlin hung from the ceiling. A ship's wheel was mounted in another window next to the X-rays. The king spoke pointed west toward the runway.

19. It was the county airport. The captain captained the whole thing. I worked in repair.

20. *You're more than we can afford* the captain said. He crossed his arms. *I can work it off* I said. *That you did is the problem* the captain said.

21. I reached for the stuffed marlin. I touched its sharp bill. *Enough* the captain said. He tore the marlin from the ceiling. He pointed it at my chest. *I can't afford more damage* the captain said. He set the marlin out of reach.

22. Quiet. *Do you realize you'll never swim again?* the captain said. *I could never swim* I said. *No sea and no salt* the captain said. I was looking out the window. Planes lifted off one after another. Amateurs. Enthusiasts. Bound by clearances. *I can't look at you* the captain said. *It's a freak thing.* He was speaking like a man in a large ship at the edge of the water staring at the end of everything. *This is it* the captain said. *I know* I said. *This is it*

23. The captain and I looked out the window and watched takeoffs and landings.

24. I crouched sick on the tarmac. The edge lights of the runway illuminated. *Let me see your hands* I heard.

25. Security. An elderly man with essential tremors. *Up* he said. *But you know me* I said. *You're a trespasser* he said.

26. We rode the length of the runway in a golf cart. We stopped at the main hangar. *This isn't the way out* I said. He unlocked the hangar doors. *Come on* he said. The plane I had been repairing was still there. Propellers spinning. I shut it off. My blood was all over the walls. He pointed to the cameras in the rafters. My blood was there too. *I saw everything that happened* he said. *No one else. Just me. I'll keep it that way too*

27. *My son was like you* he said. *But he succeeded.* He gave me his gun. *If you still want to* he said. He turned out the lights. He left me in the hangar alone with his gun. I pulled the trigger. The gun was empty.

28. *I'm glad you decided right* he said when I came back out. He wasn't alone. *Your taxi* he said.

29. The road was rough. I was knocked on my back in the backseat. The driver whistled and tapped on the steering wheel. I felt it deep in my stomach. *Please stop* I said.

30. I was thrown into the front seat. An officer tapped on the window. *Sir* the driver said. *You okay?* the officer said. *You aren't?* the driver said. *He isn't* the officer said. He pointed to the emergency lights up ahead. An upended tractor trailer. The trucker lay in pieces on the asphalt.

31. And animals. Some in cages. Some trying to run. They had been in the back of the tractor trailer before the crash. Another officer on the scene walked around and shot dead each animal one by one. *Nothing you can do?* the driver said. *Better that they not suffer* the officer said.

32. *How long do you think we're stuck here?* the driver said. *Long enough that I'd change course* the officer said. *There's no turning back now* the driver said. *They're all dead. He's dead* the officer said. *I suppose I'll pray tonight* the driver said. *Whoever claims him* the officer said. *I'll let them know you said words for him*

33. The officer shined a light on me. *Friend here don't look so good* the officer said. *Fare's paid is all that matters* the driver said. They laughed.

34. Now both officers shined lights on me. My eyes ached. I squeezed them shut. *You're not all there* the officer with the gun said. *I think I'm going to be sick* I said. *Look sick already* the officer said. *Where to you headed?* the officer with the gun said. *The rough part* the driver said. *That home for you? The rough part?* the officer said. *Yes* I said. *Are there any folks waiting up for you?* the officer with the gun said. *Will you be alone?*

35. I couldn't get past her. She was sitting in front of the door to my apartment. *Excuse me* I said. *Are you drunk?* she said. She knocked on my door. *I'm not home yet* I said. *Do you want to go home?* she said. She was speaking into my suture. *Where are you?* she said. *What happened? Was it animals? Was it teeth? Was it on purpose?* She reached for my hand. *I'm not getting through to you* she said. *Am I?*

36. She let me through. I sat with my back against the door. I felt her on the other side. I felt her through the thick of the wood. We were silhouettes. I swallowed the pills I was supposed to swallow. *Are you choking?* she said. *I hear you choking*

37. The doctor had warned me of phantoms. *Pain?* I'd said. *No* the doctor said. *That'll be real*

38. We met eyes through the crack under the door. *Let me let you in* I said. *Please?* But she was gone.

39. I followed her through the dark by feeling. I found her under a streetlight near the train yard rattling an empty cage, calling for someone. Then she was gone again.

40. I leaned my suture against a train car. Another streetlight flickered. I thought it was eyes blinking.

41. *You have to climb* she said from inside the train car. *I can't* I said. *You don't want to* she said. *I want to* I said. *Then try* she said. I reached my hand up. She took hold of me.

42. I was lifted.

43. I grunted when I hit the floor. I could smell her. I started to say something. *Shhh* she said. The train lunged forward. The train horn wailed. *We're moving* she said.

44. Morning. She lay on my arm. An animal stood over us showing me its teeth. I put distance between me and the woman. *I didn't mean for it* I said. The animal knelt beside me. *Look at yourself* the animal said. *You're harmless.* It touched my suture. *You're not okay* the animal said. *I'm trying to get better. I'm trying* I said. *Have you tried this?* the animal said. It was salt of the earth. I ate it from the animal's hand like an animal.

45. *I believe he's the same as us* she said. *In that he isn't all there in so many ways* the animal said. *Whatever was left is gone* she said. *We're going. We've gone*

46. *It's too bright in here* she said. The animal kissed her. *I have blankets* the animal said. *Too warm for blankets* she said. *I can hang them like curtains* the animal said. It draped them over the train car walls. *I've given you anything* the animal said, exhausted. It rocked her in its arms. She closed her eyes. *It's curtains* she said.

47. The animal was resting in its cage. The woman was sleeping on top of the cage. *Where are we going?* I said. *The end* the animal said. *But I never asked to be taken to the end, not like this* I said. *It isn't about asking* the animal said. *It's about taking*

48. *What do you fear?* the animal said. *I don't. I'm still a man* I said. *An incomplete man* the animal said. *Whereas I?* the animal said. *I love you* the woman said to the animal. Then she turned to me. *Do you love?* she said. *I have tried* I said.

49. *But it wasn't enough. I did not try enough*

50. Whereas they had fallen in love long ago. The wrong love. *I am no pet* the animal told animal control. But they wouldn't listen.

51. They put the animal in a cage at the aquarium. *You'll be safe here* they said. *Alive how you should be* they said. Then one night the aquarium was broken into. They broke glass. They speared fish with the shards of glass. They wrote on the walls with the insides of squids. They pocketed sharks' teeth like coins. They bent the bars of the animal's cage. They threw the animal around like it was not a life. They beat the animal. They produced a hammer and a nail and drove the nail into the animal's back.

52. And the nail shone so bright in the animal's back they fell over themselves in awe.

53. *Its throat* one of them said. Another said *Open its mouth.* They forced the animal's mouth open and readied another nail. The animal bit down, bit off their fingers. They ran. Fingerless. In pain. The animal lay in the shards of glass and the fingers until the morning. Spent.

54. *I could have escaped* the animal said. *I didn't realize it until it was too late* the animal said. Men arrived with tranquilizers and a tractor trailer. The driver strapped the animal down with all the other animals.

55. *I pulled the nail out of my own back and stabbed him with it* the animal said. *The truck crashed. I ran off while the rest of the animals were being killed*

56. *And then I found you again* she said. *I was waiting for you the entire time*

57. *for we have made a death pact for life*

58. *Just as you want to die* the animal said. *I barely escaped with my life* I said. *You did it to yourself* the animal said.

59. *I wanted it to end like this:*

60. *I decided one moment, that moment, to stick my hand out. I hoped to be caught dead.*

61. *There is no turning back now* the animal said. *We've gone*

62. *We're moving*

63. *I mean: a death pact for love or a love pact for death*

64. *Make us a family* she said. *Marry us.* The animal handed me the blankets to wear. I wrapped them around my shoulders. *I have words for you* the animal said, giving me a bible. *I don't know anything about saving* I said. *We have faith* she said. *We decided so last night. That's what's important now*

65. It was hot. The sun was bright. My hands were sweating through the pages of the bible. The ink ran. *Go on* the animal said. Smudges. *The pages are wet* I said. *Then let us be wet* they said. *I can't* I said. I threw the bible down. I tore off the blankets. *I just can't* I said. *Then stand in for me* the animal said. *But will he bite?* she said. *He's harmless* the animal said.

66. I put my arm around her. *The other too* she said. The animal shook its head. *No. I didn't mean it* she said. *Bow* the animal said.

67. The animal's sermon: *Set your hearts above things. Whatever belongs to you is coming. You once lived all things. You put on the image of all people, but it is only you now. You among you as you one another. All your hearts. Whatever you do, do it all. Submit yourselves to love. Be harsh. Embitter your hearts. Work your hearts for you.*

68. We collapsed onto each other. The woman and I. The animal straddled us like a pitchfork. *Kiss her* the animal spoke into my suture. *Kiss me* she said. I did. On the forehead.

69. The woman took hold of me and sucked at my lips until they opened. *I can taste your teeth* she said. *Where is the blood?* she said. *I want to taste blood but I don't think you've tasted any* she said. *We are wet* the animal said.

70. *I love you* she said. *I do* I said.

71. We'd been moving for days. I could see the sharps of mountains through the slits in the train car walls. The mountains turned to desert. *How much more* I said.

72. *The water is the last thing* the animal said.

73. The woman was making fish lips. She kissed the animal with her fish lips. *I will have all the fish in the water* she said. *Come water I will fill myself*

74. *And there will be oysters too. Will you feed me oysters?* she said. *All the oysters* the animal said. *I will shit shells and pearls and eat them again and again* she said. *Beautifully*

75. *And what if I wanted to keep going? What if I turned back?* I said. *You've turned back before* the animal said. *What good did it do you?*

76. *Here you are with us. Let us do it with you*

77. *But I wanted it to end like this:*

78. *There's no turning back now. You wouldn't if you could*

79. *We know this because we knew someone like you*

80. *We see us in you. Do you understand? Us?*

81. The officers heard moaning coming from the woods. They shut off their flashlights.

82. *I thought you got them all* the officer said. The officer with the gun fired into the woods. I covered my ears. Moaned.

83. We were silhouettes when she told me to take her hand and let go.

84. *Could you ever want anything more?*

85. *I am looking for you*

86. *I'm calling it off*

87. The desert turned to coast. The animal stood up. She stood up with it. We stood up.

88. I put the gun in my mouth. I pulled the trigger. The gun was empty.

89. I was afraid. I didn't say that I was afraid the only way a man should.

90. I had always been only a man.

91. *There's no turning back* the animal said, holding her close. She reached out for me.

92. *I'm still here* I said. *Aren't I?*

93. *Take our hands* they said.

94. *But I wanted it to end like this:*

95. *You've come too far to do it alone*

96. *I know* I said. I was reaching for them both. I smelled the water in their eyes.

97. We were waiting like everyone else. It wasn't how I wanted. I didn't want to wait. *I wanted it to end like this:*

98. *But there's a lot we can't do on our own*

99. We watched time pass in the shape of landscapes. Our grip tightened on each other. The water in our eyes turned thicker. The coast turned blue.

The Man with a Fish in His Heart

I HAD RUNOFF ALL OVER. I hadn't escaped the heartland. I had touched the bottom of the water with both hands and then my feet. That should have been it. But I came to in a drainage ditch at the bottom of a hill on the side of a country road. I had the bucolic sick again: the sneezing and the sunburn and the wild mushrooms you can smell through your lips. I felt siphoned. The pipe was dripping onto my stomach what had been inside my pockets when I jumped. The change hurt. I deserved it.

"You best be careful or else I'll do it," I heard spoke inside my head. I wanted it to be god. It was no god. It was a man with a gun pointed at my chest.

"I thought I was dead," I said.

"Looks like you're not from around here," he said.

"But I'm here," I said. "Aren't I?" I watched a skein of birds pass overhead. I hooked my arms around the pipe and lifted myself up.

"Don't go too far," the man said. The hammer clicked.

I looked down the road. There was no sign of anything. "Does this go east to west?" I asked.

"It goes neither far as you're concerned," the man said. He raised the gun to my head. Then he collapsed. I saw the shape of his heart beating through his chest. He was on his knees now. He pounded his chest with both fists until his heart's beating couldn't be seen anymore. He took up the gun again. "Don't look at me that way," he said. "It's just my fish."

"I think your fish wants out," I said.

The man fired into the sky. "You don't say something like that in a place you don't belong."

I put my hands up. "I didn't mean it," I lied.

"Be still," he said.

Me or the fish?

I turned toward the road. I was a hundred yards gone after two rounds. The third round went over my head and turned that skein of birds into a loss of direction. One of their bodies dropped in front of me. I jumped over it. I kept going. I was running as I had always been running. It was what I was born for like a fish in the water. The length of the road and the way it rivered through the heartland made me think this time it would be different, this time I would find the end. But it wasn't true. Because every time I think I have reached it, it isn't. I am only ever reaching.

Acknowledgments

THANK YOU to the editors, staffs, and readers of the following journals and websites, where many of these stories first appeared, including: *Adirondack Review, Black Warrior Review, Blue Mesa Review, Booth, Columbia Journal, Cosmonauts Avenue, Denver Quarterly, Devil's Lake, DIAGRAM, Front Porch Journal, Hobart, Juked, NANO Fiction, New Ohio Review, New South, Puerto Del Sol, Quarterly West,* and *Smokelong Quarterly.*

Thank you to the Northeast Ohio Master of Fine Arts program and to Cleveland State University.

Thank you to every teacher, mentor, and encourager I ever had, including: Christopher Barzak, Mary Biddinger, Sean Thomas Dougherty, Mike Geither, Frank Giampietro, David Giffels, Alissa Nutting, Caryl Pagel, and especially Imad Rahman for the introduction to this art form, and the earliest, earliest (and continuing) encouragement.

Thank you to Amber Taliancich Allen, Sarah Dravec, Anne Garwig, Amanda Howland, Genevieve Jencson, Couri Johnson, Nathan Kemp, Katie Mertz, Monica Morgan, Dan Riordan, Jessica Smith, Logan Smith, Amanda Temkiewicz, and to all the artists and writers I have been so lucky to be around and participate with in classes, workshops, readings, and so much more.

Thank you to the Ohio Arts Council for support finishing this book.

And to the many, many other incredible people (and not-people) this book owes its existence to: I haven't forgotten, won't forget, thank you.

Thank you to Christine Stroud, Mike Good, Shelby Newsom, and everybody at Autumn House Press for making this dream a book, and this book a dream.

Thank you to Pappou.

Thank you to my brothers, Anthony and Alex—thank you, Anthony and Alex.

Thank you to my grandparents, Dolly and John—thank you, Grandma and Grandpa.

Thank you to my father, Phil—thank you, Dad.

Thank you to my mother, Sandy—thank you, Mom.

And thank you, most of all, Julie. *Thank you.*

New *and* Forthcoming Releases

Heartland Calamitous by **Michael Credico**

Voice Message by **Katherine Barrett Swett** • Winner of the 2019 Donald Justice Poetry Prize, selected by Erica Dawson

The Gutter Spread Guide to Prayer by **Eric Tran** • Winner of the 2019 Rising Writer Prize, selected by Stacey Waite

Praise Song for My Children: New and Selected Poems by **Patricia Jabbeh Wesley**

under the aegis of a winged mind by **makalani bandele** • Winner of the 2019 Autumn House Poetry Prize, selected by Cornelius Eady

Hallelujah Station by **Randal O'Wain**

Grimoire by **Cherene Sherrard**

Further News of Defeat: Stories by **Michael X. Wang** • Winner of the 2019 Autumn House Fiction Prize, selected by Aimee Bender

Skull Cathedral: A Vestigial Anatomy by **Melissa Wiley** • Winner of the 2019 Autumn House Nonfiction Prize, selected by Paul Lisicky

New and Forthcoming Releases